…medes Principle

MIKE DONALD

This is a work of fiction. Names, characters, organizations, places, events, and incidents are either products of the author's imagination or are used fictitiously.

Published by BonnyMayPublishing, Oxford, United Kingdom

www.bonnymaypublishing.com

ISBN 978-1-916-1065-2-9

e-ISBN 978-1-916-1065-3-6

First Edition

Printed in the United Kingdom.

❀ Created with Vellum

For Dorrie

PROLOGUE

BARENTS SEA, DEC 13TH, 1919

The northern lights were spectacular.

A glittering curtain of iridescent light flickering across the horizon. A welcome relief from the perpetual polar night they'd endured travelling along the coast of Russia.

The crew of the *Deutschland* U-151 were taking shifts to come up on deck. The air in the sub reeked of engine oil, sweat, and fumes, from the battery room. Kapitanleutnant Helmut Schroder had decided to take a risk and surface. It was a chance for his men to spend a few minutes on deck, sucking in the crisp Arctic air, and stretching their legs.

He watched the display through the periscope,

swivelling its lens around to take in the full glory of the magical sight. And then he saw it. The unmistakable silhouette of a British warship. It sat unmoving in the ocean, a steel behemoth hunched in the gloom, waiting to strike. Maybe its captain had also decided to take in the spectacle.

And then, like two old friends locking eyes across a crowded room, Helmut realised they'd been seen.

The distant screech of the destroyer's action stations' klaxon drifted across the ocean's surface. He scrambled up the ladder into the conning tower and continued to the bridge. The men were laughing and joking as they walked around the deck, swinging their arms around to keep warm, and sharing a smoke. But the laughter soon stopped when they saw the expression on his face.

As the crew scrambled to get below, Helmut trained his Zeiss binoculars on the destroyer. Even though the war was over, it was imperative they weren't captured. Their cargo was too valuable to fall into enemy hands. The watch officer pulled the diving alarm, and the whole crew sprang into action. With the last of his crew safely below, Helmut slammed the bridge hatch, dogged it, and spun the wheel, sealing it shut. He slid down the narrow ladder from the bridge to the conning tower and gave the alarm. The bridge officer sounded the alarm bell and the crew immediately headed to their diving stations. The chief engineer shouted out the order.

'Fluten!'

The bow and stern planesmen manned their posts, putting the bow planes at maximum down angle. 'Ready to dive,' the diving officer called out. The helmsman spun the diving wheels controlling the ballast vents, while his crew pulled a series of switches and levers down one side of the cramped control room. The diesel obermaschinist threw the clutch to disengage the diesel engines as the electro obermaschinist gave the command. 'Main motors full power!' The needles of the ammeters swung into the red segments as current surged from the batteries, and the U-boat sank beneath the water.

They almost made it...

CHAPTER ONE

BRUGES, PRESENT DAY

Katja Blondell rolled onto her side and looked at the sleeping man lying next to her. She'd convinced Detective Jochum Van De Hoog she would make it worth his while spending the night at her flat rather than his barge moored in the Coupure canal.

His home was an old Euroship 1800 Luxe Motor, seized by the police as part of a drug dealer's assets and bought for peanuts by Hoog in a quixotic moment of madness. Though when they'd first met she'd found it quite romantic, the damp air and rocking motion as boats passed through the night had dampened its allure.

It was only a short walk through Astrid Park to the police station, and her friend's flat above the torture museum in Woolestraat, and she'd been working on a plan to convince him that moving in together would make sense.Katja and Jochum had become an item soon after she'd joined the Bruges police force several years earlier. It had been a whirlwind romance, and like all covert relationships between colleagues had been both exciting and frustrating due to pressure of work. But when Katja had wanted to advance her career by transferring back to Antwerp, Hoog had been less than supportive. She'd accused him of being controlling and they went through a tumultuous break-up, after which she'd left for Antwerp.

Two years later she'd been transferred back to Bruges after an ugly incident when she'd hospitalised a Japanese tourist, and the force had narrowly avoided an embarrassing court case.

Katja's boss, unaware of her previous relationship with Hoog, had suggested she be taken under his wing and brought up to speed with her public liaison skills. Their reunion in Bruges had been initially awkward, but when Hoog saved Katja and a visiting female detective from certain death in a spectacular rescue, it became obvious they were still far from over as a couple, and during the ensuing months their relationship had gone from strength to strength.

Even though Jochum was in his late thirties and five years older than her, he was in great physical shape. The low winter's sun cut like a blade through the gap in the bedroom curtains, illuminating his muscled chest as it rose and fell with his shallow breaths in front of her.

She traced the outline of his ribs with her fingertips before sliding her hand beneath the sheets. Jochum gave a low moan and his eyes flicked open. He turned his head and looked at her.

'Breaking and entering?' he said with a smile.

'I'm hoping you can help with one of those crimes,' she said. She felt him grow hard in her hand and slid over to straddle him. A rush of warmth enveloped her as he filled her with his hardness before covering her mouth with his lips. He pulled her closer and flipped her over onto her back, stroking her breasts as he increased the rhythm of his lovemaking, taking her towards a climax in what felt like seconds, but seemed to last forever, and then he shuddered, and gave a low moan.

Seconds later she matched his climax with her own, sending a wave of naked pleasure rolling through her. Jochum slid off her and took a deep breath.

'Guilty as charged,' he said. Katja pulled herself up onto one elbow.

'I'll give you time off for good behaviour,' Katja said, a smile curling across her face.

Jochum laughed. 'Give me five minutes and I might

manage a minor misdemeanour...and if that's the case, the waffles and coffee are on you.'

Hoog and Katja stood in the busy market looking across at the teeming tourists. The carillon chimed out from the 13th century medieval Belfort towering over them, and horses clattered past pulling carriages full of tourists. The sun was high, and white clouds feathered the blue sky above. It was picture perfect. But that didn't last long. An excitable young man appeared in front of them, thrusting an iPhone into Katja's hand. He spoke in broken English with an Eastern European accent.

'You take my picture, ya?' Katja looked at Hoog.

He smiled, 'Beer and chocolates,' he said. It was an expression their boss had used to remind them of the image they needed to project when dealing with members of the public. The friendly face of the law.

Katja took the iPhone from the man and angled the picture, framing the Belfort tower behind him as if he was wearing it like a pointed hat. If she had to play ball, the least she could do was give him a picture worthy of his idiocy.

She held her finger on the button until it went into

burst mode and locked up, displaying 'Out of storage.' on the screen.

Before she could hand the phone back, two men in suits appeared next to them. They would have been smartly dressed if their suits weren't a decade out of fashion. One of the men flashed a warrant card. Katja just had time to register it was an obvious fake, when the other one thrust his hand out.

'Show me your passports,' he said. Hoog shook his head. He reached into his pocket, pulled out his warrant card, and flipped it open. 'I'll show you mine if you show me yours.' The two men turned and ran, swiftly followed by the iPhone owner. Katja watched them go.'Shall we?' Hoog cricked his neck.'Why not,' Katja said.

They raced across the square after the three men. The men jostled tourists out of the way and sprinted towards a cluster of teenagers sitting on scooters, smoking, and chatting. The iPhone owner darted left, cutting down Geernaastraat, a narrow lane between two busy cafés with outside tables and striped awnings.

'Stay with the suits,' Hoog shouted.

The men reached the scooters and jumped onto two next to each other. Within seconds they were accelerating across the square and into Vlaminstraat. Hoog flashed his ID at a teenager standing next to a minuscule bright green Honda Monkey bike and jumped onto it. The teenager shook his head as Hoog started it up.

'You again? Don't you guys have cars anymore? I only just replaced the last one you smashed up.'

Hoog handed the boy a hundred euro note.

He had a point, but in times of emergency it was always better to go for the devil you knew. And as the boy had pointed out, he already knew how to ride the diminutive Honda.

'Don't worry. I'll look after it this time.'

He dropped the clutch, and the bike slewed across the cobbles. Katja watched him go, then nodded at a female student sitting on a fat-tired bicycle.

'May I?' she asked, holding up her ID. The girl shrugged and climbed off the bicycle. Katja jumped onto it and cycled across the market, past the Historium, and into Phillipstockstraat, travelling at right angles to the direction taken by Hoog.

The Honda made up for its size in power to weight ratio, and Hoog was soon gaining on the suits as they hurtled down the narrow, cobbled streets. The scooters skidded round the corner into Academiestraat, raced past the Poorterslodge, and accelerated towards Jan Van Eyck Square. They swerved around the parked cars, and then split up. One took the Spiegelrei to the left of the canal, the other the Spinolarei on the right. 'Damn!'

Hoog slid to a halt, made a split-second decision, and left a trail of rubber as he peeled left into the Spiegelrei and raced alongside the canal. Ahead of him the scooter veered across the bridge heading for the Kanaal Gent-Brugge, the main waterway encircling the city.

Hoog opened the Honda up, the rev-limiter crackling as he redlined the diminutive machine up through the gears. He was fifty feet behind the scooter, and the canal was coming up fast. The man on the scooter turned to look behind. Hoog kicked the Honda down a gear and grabbed air with the front wheel. Now level with the back of the escaping scooter, he dropped the revs, and his motorbike slammed down onto the driver's back. The scooter catapulted past a left turn, skidded over the towpath, and plunged into the canal. Hoog slammed on his brakes, slid to a halt, and jumped off his bike. The man in the suit thrashed around in the water, yelling, his face contorted with fear.

'I can't swim...help!' 'Shit!' Hoog said.

He shrugged off his coat and shoes, dropped his cell, keys, and wallet onto his jacket and ran down to the edge of the canal.

Katja cycled along Philipstockstraat parallel to the Burg, winding through the narrow, cobbled streets before joining Hoogstraat, heading for the canal. She flicked a look at her cell phone and smiled, before slipping it back into her pocket. Minutes later she was crossing the canal and taking a left into Molenmeers, passing Jeruzalemkerk, an ancient 15th-century church. The church had acquired a kind of notoriety when its crypt featured in the film *In Bruges* as a stand in for the Basilica of the Holy Blood. She reached the junction that doglegged into Speelmansstraat opposite Carmersstraat and pulled up.

CHAPTER TWO

Hoog watched as a tall officer with a severe haircut and his colleague placed the man in the mud-covered suit into the back of the patrol car. They'd brought Hoog some fresh clothes from his locker at the station, for which he'd been grateful. A small crane like a steel spider lifted the scooter out of the canal and lowered it onto the path. The tall officer went over to it and opened one of the panniers. He fished out something and dropped it into an evidence bag.

He came over to Hoog and held up the bag, which contained two passports.

'Looks like a slow day on the passport front.'

'Do you have a spare pair of gloves?' Hoog asked. The officer handed him some disposable gloves.

'Thanks.' Hoog put them on and pointed at the bag.

‘Can I?’ The officer handed him the bag. Hoog pulled the soggy passports out and peeled them open.

‘A reasonable likeness,’ he said.

‘You think he was planning on using them himself?’ the tall officer asked.

‘I don’t know. Normally the thieves just steal them and doctor the photographs. But it’s getting much harder with the latest passports.’

‘Hey! Have a look at this.’ The other officer beside the scooter called out. Hoog went over and looked into the pannier. A dull yellow slab of metal lay inside. He peered down at it. To all intents and purposes, it looked like a gold ingot. He reached in and lifted it out. It was old and bore some distinctive marks on it. He ran his fingers over the indentations. He’d seen them before.

‘It looks Russian. You better take that back to the station. And I wouldn’t make any stops on the way just in case it’s the real thing.’ The tall officer took the ingot and hefted it in his hand before putting it carefully into an evidence bag.

‘Feels like the real thing. I’ll look after it, and we’ll send you a card from Barbados.’

‘For sure,’ Hoog said.

The tall officer put the evidence bag with the gold bar into the car boot and slammed it shut. He turned to Hoog. 'You need a lift?' Hoog shook his head. 'Naa. I've got to return the bike anyway.' The officer nodded.

'Okay. Anything from Katja?' Hoog shook his head. 'You know what she's like. She'll turn up.'

The officer climbed into the patrol car, and started it up before lowering the window.

'We've put an alert out for the other scooter.'

'Thanks,' Hoog said. The officer gave him a nod, and drove off. Hoog's cell buzzed from inside his jacket. He pulled it out and tapped the screen. Katja's voice came out of the speaker. 'How's it going?' she asked.

'The guy in the suit ended up in the canal. The idiot couldn't swim.' Hoog imagined Katja smiling as she heard that. 'Just your luck,' she said.

'Do you need a lift? I could piggyback you on the bike,' Hoog said. He heard what sounded like a snort coming through the speaker.

Then, 'Let me think about that. Mmmm, squashed against a damp man on a tiny bike. No, I'm good.'

Hoog looked down at his dishevelled state before replying, 'Fair point.'

'I'll let you know if I get eyes on the other suit,' she paused, then, 'I could murder a Bagel. I'd forgotten what hard work cycling was,' Katja said.

'Did you say cycling?' Hoog asked. 'Gotta' go,' Katja said, and the call cut off.

CHAPTER THREE

Katja ducked down and pretended to check her bike tires. The sound of an approaching scooter grew louder and seconds later the other man in a suit appeared. He slowed down and parked up alongside the wall bounding the folk museum next to some bicycles. Katja watched as he chained the scooter to a steel bollard. *Yes, you don't want to take any chances, a lot of crooks live round here,* she thought.

The man looked around, and Katja kept her head turned away from him. Satisfied that no one was following him, he headed down the street towards a small, whitewashed house. He stopped, reached into his pocket and pulled out some keys. He was about to insert them into the lock when Katja caught up with him.

'Hello again,' she said, showing him her ID. 'You still in the passport game?'

The man gave a sick grin and launched a flying punch at her with his whole body weight behind it, which was a good thing as far as Katja was concerned. She leaned to the right, and grabbed the man's traveling arm, adding her momentum to it. He flew across the narrow street, his body slamming against the whitewashed wall opposite.

He gave a low grunt, leaving a smear of blood on the wall before standing up on wobbly legs. Katja looked at him.

'Do you really want to do this?' she asked. The man ran towards her, arms flailing. She threw out a leg, pivoting round and out of his way as he passed. Her leg smashed into his back, slamming him into the wall for the second time. She heard a dull crunch as he took the impact on his nose. He turned around, touched his nose, and stared at the blood on his hand. It didn't take long for this genius to work out it was broken.

'Bitch!' He spat blood onto the cobbles and tried to focus. *This would be a good time to come quietly*, Katja thought. But he didn't. And now he had a knife in his hand. Katja went into a low crouch, circling, keeping him off balance. He'd already had enough opportunity to avoid hospital food, and the knife had added attempted murder onto the passport theft and impersonating a police officer charge. It was time to shut him down. He ran towards her. His knife arm stretched out in front of him. He was planning on using his brute strength to drive the blade through her, pinning her like a butterfly into the garage door behind. But that wasn't going to happen. Not today. She let him come forward, cross blocked his knife arm, twisted his arm around, and joint locked his elbow.

He had two choices. Drop the knife or end up with a dislocated elbow. There was a dull crunch as he made the wrong choice. He gave a high-pitched scream and dropped the knife. Katja kicked it across the cobbles before bringing out her cuffs and linking his good arm to his ankle. He sat on the ground glaring at her. She took out her cell and tapped the screen. Waited for it to connect.

'Detective Katja Blondell. I need transport and medical assistance to 43 Rolweg. The suspect has a broken nose and a fractured or dislocated elbow.' She listened. 'No, I'm fine.' She ended the call and slipped the cell into her pocket. She looked down at the injured man.

'Okay, you have a choice here. You can end up in prison for a long time for the attempted murder of a police officer. Or, you could tell us who you're working for and spend less time inside for impersonating a police officer, possession of a deadly weapon, and theft. What works best for you?'

CHAPTER FOUR

Hoog sat across from Katja at the Sanseveria Bagelsalon, in Predikherenstraat. He was wolfing down a bagel and occasionally taking a slug of strong coffee. He watched as Katja took a more leisurely approach to her food. He'd been caught out too many times in mid-meal by some sort of emergency call-out, and liked to get his food down as fast as possible. They were still enveloped in the bubble of adrenalin from the pursuit, and needed to draw a line under their aggression. A bagel and a cake were their go-to drugs of choice. He took another sip of coffee to wash the bagel down and shook his head. 'I can't believe you commandeered a bicycle to chase after a crook on a scooter.'

'It's not about speed. You were the hare, and I was

the tortoise. Besides, I had the advantage of knowing where he was going to end up.'

'I was convinced they were using false plates, otherwise, I would have called their registrations in,' Hoog said.

'Thieves are more likely to clone plates these days. I took a chance that those guys weren't smart enough to have bothered about their plates. After all, they would be on foot most of the time.'

'You got lucky,' Hoog said.

'That's me, lucky Blondell,' Katja said with a smile. Hoog looked around. The owner, Bert, played jazz music which, combined with the décor, gave the place a hipster vibe. He'd ordered a "Leon," a breakfast bagel with scrambled egg and smoked salmon, and it was taking all his skill to avoid dropping it on his shirt. He took a sip of his coffee and another bite of the bagel.

'This is good,' he said between mouthfuls, wiping his lips before speaking. 'That passport scam has been running for a while now.'

Katja bit into her bagel and swallowed before replying. 'Yes. If we can get one of them to cough up a name it might give us a lead to the head of the operation, and we can shut them down. Then I can start packing.'

They were both looking forward to joining their new colleagues, English detective Chandler Travis along with Louisiana sheriff Duke Lanoix, and his forensic assistant

Roxie Rosedale. Chandler and his American colleagues had travelled to Bruges to assist them with a case co-ordinated by Europol. The discovery of a headless torso in the canal next to the police station had revealed similarities to their recent case in Louisiana and Hoog had made a request for them to join the investigation.

As the case progressed they had bonded as a team. Their investigation stretched back to 19th century London, and involved Jack the Ripper, conspiracies in the Louisiana oil fields, and corruption at the highest levels of government. Duke and Chandler's investigation out in Louisiana had led them to a New Orleans Voodoo queen named Marsha Brochell, who had links to Louisiana Governor Roman Blackburn, a prime suspect in the Ripper case of 1888. They discovered that a descendant of Marsha Brochell's was behind the events in Bruges, and that the planting of the torso had been used to draw Travis and Duke, along with Roxie, into her web. Even though Marsha's attempted revenge on them for the death of her lover Roman Blackburn out in Louisiana had failed, the diversion had allowed her to accomplish her secondary aim of stealing the Holy Blood relic from the basilica. The theft, and the subsequent discovery that Marsha and her accomplice had gone to ground in Venice, had set in motion a "whatever it costs" mission to track them down and recover the relic. The Holy Blood relic was a big tourist draw, and their cover story about it being cleaned would only hold for so long. With Europol once more co-ordinating the various departments, Duke, Chandler and Roxie were already in Venice, and Hoog and Katja were anxious to wrap up their recent case and join them in the city of water. Hoog took another mouthful of his bagel. 'I expect you'll be adding a pair of waterproof boots to your wardrobe the way things are going over there?' Katja gave him a tight smile. The floods had worsened in Venice, and the tourist trade had taken a hit. With St Mark's square regularly underwater, moving around would be difficult.

Katja sipped her coffee. 'It's not going to make their job any easier over there, that's for sure.'

Hoog's mobile vibrated on the table next to him. It was their new Police Chief, Nils Janssen. Hoog picked it up. 'Chief?'

He listened. 'Okay, we'll see you shortly,' He put the phone down. Katja could tell from his expression that it wasn't good news.

"What?'

He sighed. 'We might have to hold off on the packing for a bit.'

CHAPTER FIVE

They sat opposite Chief Nils Janssen back at the station, their eyes drawn to the object that took pride of place in the middle of his desk. The dull metal gleamed under the cold fluorescent lights. Katja studied the Russian markings on the heavy ingot in front of her, her eyes sparkling with curiosity. 'I've heard a lot about the Romanov gold, but I've never seen the real thing,' she said. The gold brick lay there, four hundred ounces, roughly 25 pounds or 11 and a half kilos. Either way, it was worth a small fortune, and if it was an authentic Romanov ingot, it could open up a can of political worms. Katja felt her trip to the romantic city of Venice running away from her faster than a dog with a sausage in a butcher's shop.

'How do you think it ended up in the hands of a petty criminal?' Janssen asked.

'We haven't officially interviewed him yet, but at the moment, he denies it's anything to do with him,' Hoog said.

Katja smiled, 'it's hardly likely that somebody planted it on him.'

Janssen stared at the gold. 'You and Hoog interview him, and I'll get the ingot tested. We need to know if this is for real or a fake, before we take things any further.'

Hoog reached out to the gold bar, his hand hovering over it. 'Has it been processed?' Janssen grunted. 'For sure, no prints,' he replied. Hoog hefted it in his hand, looked at the markings, and put it back down.

Katja looked at it sitting on the desk. 'So how much is it worth?' she asked.

Janssen tapped on a calculator, frowned. 'If it's real, nearly half a million euros. Give or take.'

Katja looked at Hoog. 'So why was he pulling some low-level passport scam?''Maybe he was planning on leaving the country in a hurry and needed a new passport,' Hoog said.

Katja reached over and touched the gleaming ingot with her fingertips. She'd read some of the many conspiracy theories surrounding the disappearance of the Romanov gold.

Along with its mythology, there was a reason why the whereabouts of the gold might remain a secret even if its hiding place was discovered.

The appearance of such a large amount of Russian gold would trigger an ugly confrontation between the Russian state, descendants of Tsar Nicholas II, and other nations, including Britain, who would claim they were owed outstanding debts by the fallen Romanov dynasty. Along with the political ramifications, dumping such a vast amount of gold onto the market would plunge the gold markets into chaos.

Janssen stood up before speaking. 'If it is real, and there's more, we could be looking at a political shit-storm. But let's not get into that right now. Set up an interview with them, and let's see what they have to say.'

Katja and Hoog got up. Katja pointed at the gold. 'Do you want us to look after that?' Janssen smiled. 'Very funny.'

He picked the gold bar up and went over to a small safe set into the wall at one end of his office. He spun the dial backwards and forwards, then slid the bar inside before closing the door and twisting the combination.

CHAPTER SIX

Katja and Chief Janssen watched through the one-way mirror, looking into the interview room. Hoog sat opposite the man in the suit he'd pulled out of the canal. The suit had given them his name, Jacobus Bakker. But so far, that was the extent of his conversation. His lawyer sat impassively as Bakker repeated his interminable mantra of 'No comment' to Hoog's questions. They'd already questioned Xander Sven, the man Katja had arrested, as he was treated for his injuries in hospital, with the same results.

Janssen turned to Katja. 'Did you find anything on them?'

Katja shrugged. 'We have their addresses, driver's licenses and names, so we know where they live. Bakker has a criminal record but hasn't served any time.'

Janssen turned to her. 'What for?' Janssen said.

'Fake antiques, illegal imports, nothing major.'

'Okay. Well, let me know if you get anything out of them. We'll keep the gold out of the report for now.''Couldn't we just pass this over to the Feds?' Katja said.

'Too early for that, but I understand your reluctance to take on the case. I know you're keen to join your foreign colleagues.' Janssen said.

'Yes, they're going to need all the help they can get,' Katja said. 'Well, let's hope this is a one-off, and he just got unlucky when he bumped into you two,' Janssen said as he headed out of the room, leaving Katja staring through the glass.

Hoog ran his hand through his hair and took a long slow breath. The interview with Bakker and his attorney was going nowhere fast. Hoog had decided that Bakker was the brains of the outfit, such as they were, and needed to break the stalemate. Bakker owned a couple of antique shops in Predikherenstraat specializing in expensive objet d'art, high-end furniture, and old paintings.

Maybe once they'd conducted a search of his shops, they'd have more leverage in an interview, and God forbid, they might even get some evidence.

He decided to try a little fishing with Bakker. He leaned forwards. 'If we took a look around your business premises, do you think we might find any more precious metals?' Bakker started to say 'No comment,' but stopped himself. A sheen of sweat had begun to form on his upper lip. He wiped it away with his hand before replying. 'I already told you, I don't know anything about the gold.'

'Okay, so you want us to believe that somebody decided that the best place to hide half a million euros' worth of gold bullion was in your scooter pannier.

Bakker shrugged. 'Why would I be involved in some petty passport scam if I had a half a million euro's worth of gold stashed in my scooter?' Hoog smiled. 'I don't know, maybe it has the same logic you applied when you pretended you couldn't swim. We know from your record that you worked as a commercial diver on the Blauwwind windfarm project.' Bakker's beady eyes narrowed. 'I was just messing with you,' Bakker said. Hoog sighed. 'Okay, I love a good joke, so why don't we have you taken back to a comfy cell for 24 hours while you see if you can find something more amusing to talk about. Bakker leaned over and said something into his attorney's ear. The attorney nodded. 'You need to get a search warrant,' Bakker said.

Hoog stood up. 'Thanks for sharing your incisive grasp of the legal system. But because of your love of answering "No Comment" to our questions, I took the precaution of applying for one several hours ago. I imagine that by tomorrow we will have more to talk about.' Hoog left the interview room as two of his officers came to escort Bakker to the cells.

Katja was waiting for him. 'What now?' she asked.

'We take a look around his premises.'

CHAPTER SEVEN

They edged past a group of white police vans lining the pavement outside the antique and interior design shops sitting opposite each other in Predikheren-straat. The interior consisted of a series of twisting corridors crowded with dusty pictures, objet d'art, and small pieces of antique furniture. They squeezed past CSI officers taking pictures and logging items of possible interest. At the end of one corridor, they reached an industrial space with a skylight that added a grey light to the harsh overhead fluorescents. There were some oxy-acetylene welding rigs, wooden crates, drums of chemicals and piles of tools scattered around.

'This place goes on forever,' Hoog said, looking around. 'Yes. Reminds me of Stef Antiek's in Rue Blaes,' Katja said. Hoog knew the area she was talking about well. Rue Blaes was an area in old Brussels packed with antique shops and usually crowded with tourists after a bargain. Stef's Antiek's had thousands of different items, piled high against the walls and hanging from the roof. Situated in the Kapellemarkt, the site of Napoleon's old stables, it had thousands of antique chairs, retro lamps, and antique building materials, with so much to go at you could easily refurbish an entire house from the ground up.

'As an antique dealer, if that's what he is, it does give him a perfect cover for moving goods around the world under the pretence of import-export,' Katja said.

Hoog looked around. 'That's for sure.' Hoog went over to one of the wooden crates and studied the labels on the lids.

Katja joined him. 'Bakker is a man of many talents... looks like he's a potter as well as a thief, commercial diver, and antique dealer.' Katja tapped the label on one of the crate's lids. 'Magnesium Oxide...' she moved to the next container. 'Ethyl Silicate, Barium Titanate, Ammonium Sulphide. All components used in the manufacturer of ceramics and sculptures.'

'How come you know so much about pottery? Hoog said.

'At my school, you had a choice. You could either do sports, or some kind of art like painting, or pottery.'

'So, you chose pottery to get out of doing hockey.

'That's for sure, but I hated pottery. All those spotty boys making ugly clay ashtrays.'

Hoog smiled. I can't see Bakker working on the potter's wheel myself. What else could those chemicals be used for?'

Katja pointed at the chemical crates. 'Ceramic is used in lost wax casting.'

Hoog looked at her. 'That sounds mysterious.'

'It's a process used to cast duplicate metal sculptures, often silver, gold, brass or bronze from an original sculpture.'

'Why's it called lost wax?' Hoog asked.

'It starts with a wax carving, which forms the positive. A ceramic slurry is then poured over it to form a negative mould. Once that has set, the molten metal is poured into the mould causing the wax to melt and drain away.'

'So, the wax disappears, or is lost?'

'Yes. The ceramic outer shell is then removed to reveal the metal cast to be finished, or assembled, if it's constructed using a series of separate parts.'

'It's a far more complicated process than I imagined,' Hoog said.

'And expensive. If you wanted to have a bronze cast of yourself it could cost you around fifty thousand euros.'

Hoog shook his head. 'That's not going to happen.'

Detective Ward came over to them. Recently promoted to detective he'd become a valuable member of the team and was a specialist when it came to IT matters and cybercrime.

'Anything suspicious?' Hoog asked.

'It's like looking for a needle in a haystack in this place,' Ward said, before continuing.

'Obviously, it would be great if we found evidence of a forging operation or a hidden cellar packed with Romanov gold.' Katja laughed. She'd always liked Ward's deadpan humour, and along with Hoog, she'd been badly shaken when he'd nearly drowned in the catacombs beneath the police station.

'I'm guessing that's not the case?' Katja said. Ward shook his head. 'No. If he'd had a mobile phone on him, that would have helped us track his movements before his arrest. But I did find something interesting in his import/export records.' 'Go on,' Hoog said.

Ward continued. 'Well, under the RGR, returned goods relief law, goods exported and re-imported within three years generally get total or partial relief from customs duty. Which is relevant to my next bit of info.'

'I'm all ears,' Hoog said.

'Looking at his list of exported and re-imported antiques, the majority of goods listed are repeated on a regular basis,' Ward waited.

'It's strange, but it's not illegal. He's just moving stuff around,' Katja said.

'I agree, but it looks like he's taking the same goods and failing to sell them each time.' Katja thought about this. 'You think he's transporting something in amongst the artefacts, or in them? Drugs?'

'Forensics are testing for traces of drugs in anything hollow that has been regularly exported and re-imported. So far, nothing has turned up.'

'How about traces of gold?' Katja asked.

'That was my second thought. Nothing so far,' Ward said.

Hoog wandered over to the crates of chemicals. 'Have these been checked?'

Ward looked up. 'For sure. The chemicals are what it says on the crates.'

Hoog pried open the lid of one of the chemical crates. He reached in with a gloved hand, and sifted through the white powder.'

Ward looked at him. 'It's not cocaine, we already checked.'

Hoog smiled. 'I think I'd probably recognize that smell.' His hand stopped moving. He reached in with his other hand and after a bit of a struggle, pulled out a rectangular lump of metal. He brushed off the powder, and they saw the dull gleam of a familiar gold bar. He laid it carefully on top of a nearby crate. 'We'd better get the boys to check all of these crates in case there are any more,' Katja said. Hoog picked up the gold ingot and hefted it in his hands.

'What is it?' Katja asked.

'Well, compared to the one in Chief Janssen's safe, this one's a lot heavier.'

'Could the other bar be a fake?' Ward asked.

'Shouldn't take too long to find out,' Hoog said.

Ward looked around the massive piles of antiques and architectural pieces. 'The whole Romanov gold thing is an Alice in Wonderland rabbit hole, and the history of the Russian empire is not one of my areas of expertise. But I know someone who lives and breathes history...'

Katja smiled. She knew exactly who he meant. 'Erika?'

Ward nodded. 'I've sent her all the information we have along with pictures of the original ingot and the markings. She's collating the various myths and news items surrounding the gold's disappearance from Siberia in the aftermath of the Bolshevik revolution back in 1919. She may have some thoughts as to where the gold originated from.'

'Well, I'm sure they've got things under control here, why don't we head over to the museum and see what she can tell us.'Maybe get a coffee on the way,' Hoog said as they headed out of the shop.

'I'm surprised you ever get any sleep, the amount of coffee you pour down your neck,' Katja said.

'You know me too well. But I try and limit myself to three cups a day,' Hoog said.

'Right, I'm the same with cakes,' Katja said.

CHAPTER EIGHT

They sat at a table in front of. the 't Santpoortje bar overlooking 't Zand, Bruges' largest public square. It had once been populated by a collection of bronze fountain sculptures depicting cycling, the landscapes of Flanders, fishermen, and bathing women symbolising the towns of Bruges, Ghent, Antwerp, and Kortrijk. But in 2018, the statues were stolen from a storage facility before they could be moved to their new site at King Albert I park. Taken by a gang of metal thieves, the statues were never recovered.

Hoog took a sip of his coffee before turning to Katja. 'I was hoping this case would be over quickly so we could join our friends across the water,' Hoog said.

'Me too,' Katja said, taking a sip of coffee. 'Let's hope we can get some answers from our friends down at the station. I'm already starting to suffer from a lack of gondolas and pasta in my life.'

Hoog nibbled at the small biscuit that had accompanied his coffee. 'Worst case scenario we charge them with what we've got.'

Katja put her cup down. 'Theft, grievous bodily harm and assaulting a police officer...maybe attempted murder. It'll drag on. And if more gold turns up...' she left it hanging.

'If there's more gold, the Feds might take over, and then we can pack our waterproofs and get over there.' Hoog slid a twenty euro note under his saucer and waved at the waiter. They walked out of the square and back into town, heading for the Groeninge Museum, where Erika worked as a curator.

CHAPTER NINE

Hoog and Katja stood beside Erika and Ward in Erika's cramped office at one end of the Groening museum's storage area. Some printouts from the internet and a series of photos were tacked to a corkboard on one of the walls. She'd drawn arrows and dates with a felt tip on the A4 sheets to form a crude timeline linking the various Romanov myths and relevant newspaper articles.

There was a bewildering collection of theories and articles dating back to the fall of the Romanov empire during the Russian revolution of 1917. Ward was busy on his laptop completing a file upload.

'The internet connection's not great in here, so while we're waiting, why don't you tell us what you know about the Romanovs.' Though she was in her eighties there wasn't much, if anything, Erika couldn't talk about from a historical perspective. Her years as a curator at the Groeninge museum, immersed amongst the ancient artefacts and paintings, had given her a unique view into the past.

'What I know about the Romanovs would fill a book, but I think what you really want to hear is, where's the gold?'

Ward smiled. 'If you knew that, I imagine we would be having this conversation in the Erika Van Houston-Vinke museum.'

'Yes indeed. But let me give you some historical context, if we're to narrow down the myths surrounding where it might have ended up,' Erika said.

'An overview will do, Erika; we have a couple of criminals cooling their heels that we need to sort out if we're ever going to Venice,' Hoog said.

Erika shuffled through her printouts. 'Very well. The value of the Russian imperial family with all of its jewelry, gold, cash, land and palaces was around 40 billion euros when the House of Romanov fell in 1917.'

Katja leaned forwards. 'So where did it all go?'

'Well, the simple explanation is that the Bolsheviks stole most of it.'

'I'm guessing it's not that simple,' Hoog said.

'No, they may have got their hands on some of it, but a fortune in gold and jewelry is still unaccounted for. But for each bar of gold there's another story of where it might have ended up.' Erika showed them a picture of the Tsar, his Empress Alexandra, their four Princess daughters, and his son and heir Alexei.'

'What a beautiful family,' Katja said, entranced by the picture.

'Yes, they were. But in July 1918, they were executed in Yekaterinburg,' she paused, and then went on.'The family had a fortune in diamonds sewn into the underclothes of the Grand Duchesses, a cruel irony that only prolonged their deaths.'

'I remember reading an article about that.' Katja said.

'The bullets ricocheted off the diamonds when they were shot, and they had to be finished off with bayonets and rifle butts,' she shivered at the images that flashed into her mind. 'All of their wealth and beauty had conspired against them.' Erika put the photo down. 'Yes. A tragic end indeed.' Hoog picked up the photo and looked to Erika. 'So, then what happened?'

'Well, in the aftermath of the Bolshevik revolution a huge amount of the Tzar and his family's treasure went missing. So, let's look at the various theories and see if we can find anything that might explain how your petty thief and antique dealer got his hands on some of that Romanov gold over a hundred years later, if it's the real thing, of course.' 'We're waiting to hear from Heidi in forensics on that,' Katja said.

Erika smiled and moved over to the wall of pictures. 'Some people think the gold was buried out in the woods, or at the bottom of a lake. One of the more interesting theories concerns Kolchak's Gold Train, an armoured train carrying hundreds of tons of gold bullion and roubles. That story begins in Russia.'

CHAPTER TEN

TATARSKAYA, RUSSIA 1919

Fireman Sergei Kuznetzov warmed his hands in front of the flaming jaws of the firebox as they thundered through the night. They were driving an old Baltic type four-cylinder, 4-6-4 compound locomotive. It had been abandoned in the Omsk marshalling yards awaiting repair. Sergei had managed to patch it up and they'd been using it as a 'banking' engine at the rear of the train.

It had been essential to help them navigate the many long, steep gradients along the Trans-Siberian Railway on their way to Irkutsk. Because of its low number of wheels, it had poor tractive adhesion, but that didn't matter now, because its speed on the level was what they needed. Beside him, engineer Dimitri Bolshov stared into the darkness ahead. He could make out the distant shape of the rear carriage attached to Kolchak's gold train, and the glimmer of train D's running lights. They were a few miles outside of Tatarskaya station and their timing was critical. As far as anybody knew, train D was hauling a fortune in gold ingots and roubles. But Dimitri and Sergei knew different.

The lights of Tatarskaya town glimmered in the distance.

'Are you ready?' Dimitri asked. Sergei nodded. 'Let's hope we kill Kolchak and some of his Cossack bastards.' Dimitri understood the reason for Sergei's hatred. His entire family had been murdered when Cossack warlords had burned his village down during the peasant uprisings.

Dimitri had no love for Kolchak, but they weren't there for revenge. Their mission was far more important than that. Dimitri reached forwards and pulled the brass handle controlling the regulator valve, sending more steam into the cylinders.

He saw the '*white feather*', a puff of steam against the night sky as the safety valve vented, and the locomotive picked up speed. He adjusted the damper and boosted the air flow into the firebox. He flicked a look at the glass steam pressure gauge which was nudging 150 psi, and turned to Sergei.

'Pressure's good.' The distant shape of the station

loomed out of the darkness. Dimitri looked at Sergei. 'Get ready. One, two...three!'

They jumped clear of the train, landing in the high grass beside the track. Dimitri picked himself up and stood watching, as the locomotive thundered towards the station.

They jogged back through the darkness beside the track until they reached the abandoned repair depot where the U-120 locomotive and its five armoured carriages sat hissing, a dark shape hunched in the gloom. They'd left it idling to avoid the hours it would have taken for the engine to come up to pressure in the freezing conditions.

They climbed into the cab and Dimitri eased the brass-handled steam regulator open. The pressure increased in the glass and he released the brakes. The locomotive lurched beneath them, the heavy steel wheels slipping on the freezing rails before gripping the tracks. The locomotive edged forward, its massive pistons forcing the wheels round, easing the engine out of the repair depot and back onto the main line. As they picked up speed an enormous explosion lit up the sky, criss-crossing the night with flashes of light. They heard the staccato crack of detonating munitions echoing down the line. Sergei gave a grim smile before speaking. 'We'll take the spur link round the station. It'll take them weeks to repair the main line, and by then we'll be long gone.' Dimitri wasn't looking forward to the thousands of kilometres they would have to cover before they reached their rendezvous at Lake Baikal. He fumbled in his pocket and produced a battered hip flask. He unscrewed the top and held it out to Sergei. 'Medovukha, it's the best I can do. Don't tell anyone where you got it from.' Sergei smiled, took the flask and slugged down a mouthful before handing it back. 'I don't think we need to worry about being caught with alcohol.''That is true comrade; after all, we just blew up Admiral Kolchak's gold train.'

CHAPTER ELEVEN

The setting sun wounded the surface of the ice with a blood red scar. The crescent shape of Lake Baikal covered over 31,000 square kilometres and was 635 kilometres long and 78 kilometres wide. With a depth of over 1600 metres, it was the deepest freshwater lake in the world. Now, in the height of winter, the water was frozen to a depth of two metres. The clarity of the ice was such that it was possible to look down into its depths for over 40 metres.

Sergei could see the swirling patterns of bubbles corkscrewing upwards through the ice...frozen like a giant fairy-tale Princess's pearl necklace, while other bubbles trapped in the ice stretched up from the depths like strings of frozen mushrooms.

As a child Sergei's father had taken him onto the

lake beneath where he stood, and pointed out the remains of an old truck that had misjudged the thickness of the ice in its attempt to cross the lake. Legend had it that for many years, and only when the ice was at its clearest, the body of the driver could be seen clinging to the steering wheel in the cab, his face frozen in the rictus grimace of his icy death. Even as an innocent child Sergei had thought that this part of the legend was designed to frighten people, and to make sure no one took any chances when crossing the lake.

Sergei wasn't taking any chances that night. He looked across the shimmering ice stretching out below and braced himself for the task ahead. At over twenty-five million years old, Lake Baikal held many secrets, and after that nights' endeavours it would hold another one close to its icy breast.

Sergei tilted his binoculars down to the shore below. He could see the flickering pinpricks of light from the small fires his team were clustered round to ward off the bitter chill. As they'd hoped, the wind was picking up. Against the fading light he could make out the silhouettes of the fifty or more boats that sat upon the ice beneath him. Originally built to sail across water, they had been modified for tonight's enterprise.

Using a combination of old horse drawn ploughs and dog sleds, the boats had been converted to travel over the fifty miles of ice that lay between Tolsty Cape and their destination at Turukhit Bay.

The ice would support up to fifteen tons within each vessel, so Sergei's calculations had to be as accurate as possible or the consequences would be catastrophic. In very cold winters, when the ice was too thick for the ice-breakers, temporary rail tracks would have been laid across the ice and the carriages would be pulled by oxen or horses. But with the civil war raging, the lake was barren of any such tracks.

The men had constructed a steep chute made of animal feeding troughs with the ends cut off. Joined together and coated with water that immediately froze, they formed a crude delivery system to channel the ingots of gold from the railway carriages down the rocky embankment to the men waiting by the ice-boats.

He looked back at the dark shape of the U-120 locomotive and its five carriages. The first part of their plan had worked well, and they had the gold. The explosion and the fire that raged through Tatarskaya station when the locomotive hit would have left gold bullion and roubles scattered across the tracks, adding to the confusion over the missing gold. It would take weeks to unravel the chaos, and by then the gold would be safely across Lake Baikal and headed for the Russian coast.

CHAPTER TWELVE

The surface of the ice reflected the full moon gleaming overhead. From his vantage point high above the lake, Sergei could see fish flickering through the water beneath the crystal-clear ice, and for one brief moment thought he could make out the dark shadow of the sunken truck.

He heard the crunch of gravel behind him and turned to see a motley group of men, maybe twenty or more, heading along the railway track towards him. They were swathed in the thickest clothes they could find to protect them from the freezing wind. One man towered over the rest; his name was Igor and he was over six foot five with a vast black beard spilling down from his square chin. They would need all the muscle they could get to unload the gold ingots from the train carriages, each of the heavy gold bars would be like shifting a weightlifter's dumbbell.

Sergei had decided that they would work until dawn and leave enough gold bars and roubles in the carriages to give the impression that the missing gold was spread across the bottom of Lake Baikal.

By forming a human chain from the carriage to the lip of the chute, he calculated they should be able to load around six bars a minute. By changing over each group of ten men every half hour, he estimated they should be able to send around 250 ingots down to the waiting boats per hour. The people on the shore who were stacking and loading the gold had a harder job.

Loading the ingots onto the waiting ice-boats had taken all night. But in the winter the nights were long, and before dawn arrived the small flotilla of converted boats began their trip across the ice to Turukhit Bay. There was only one boat waiting for Dimitri down below. What he had to do next was essential if they were to cover their tracks.

Dimitri climbed onto the footplate of the U-120 and hauled himself into the cab. The locomotive weighed over seventy tons and had a top speed of over 100 kilometres an hour, though most of their journey had been at a crawl due to the weight of their cargo, the steep gradients and the freezing temperatures.

Dimitri looked around at the brass levers and dials that had been part of his life for so long. He rested his hand on the regulator levers that controlled the fuel and air feeding into the firebox beneath the boiler that provided the steam to power the steel colossus.

As a young boy his father had let him ride in the cab of the engine and even allowed him to sound the whistle as they approached the station or a sharp bend. But that was long ago, before his father had been executed by an officer of Cheka, the soviet secret police, for supposed anti-communist sympathies. It was one of the reasons Dimitri's allegiance had switched to the German cause and he had joined the *Moon Wolves* movement. With the execution of the Romanovs, and the seizure of their enormous wealth, a fortune in gold, platinum and roubles had ended up under Admiral Kolchak's control in Omsk. As the civil war raged throughout Russia, and the Red Forces advanced, Kolchak decided to move his political and military base further east to Irkutsk. This meant transporting and protecting the gold reserves along the Trans-Siberian railway.

As Admiral Kolchak's gold trains were being amassed

in the marshalling yards of Omsk, Sergei and Dimitri had seen a chance to make Germany a great empire once more.

Kolchak's gold train consisted of forty armoured goods wagons and their locomotives, formed into five trains labelled A, B, C, D and E, with the gold carried in train "D". Dimitri and Sergei knew that as the Fifth Red Army advanced on Omsk, chaos would inevitably ensue, as people fled the city. Their plan had to be put into operation as soon as possible. Rather like a street trickster who asks the public to guess which shell the coin is under, they would have to use sleight of hand to achieve their aim.

The gold train was being protected by a small detachment of White Army troops. Cold, hungry and bone weary, they had been guarding the carriages containing the gold for months and their interest in them was now minimal.

The marshalling yards of Omsk were massive, packed with thousands of abandoned rail carriages, rusted locomotives and armoured cargo carriages. They'd been left to rot as the normal business of transporting goods had come to a grinding halt beneath the onslaught of the Russian civil war.

Sergei and Dimitri soon located what was needed if their shell game was to succeed. A group of five empty armoured goods carriages, identical to those containing the gold being guarded by the White Army troops. All they had to do was swap the identification plates on the gold train carriages with the empty armoured carriages and make off with the spoils.

CHAPTER THIRTEEN

In the weeks leading up to the departure of Kolchak's gold train, Sergei and Dimitri had used their locomotive to shunt the various carriages into position as the five trains were assembled and prepared for their journey to Irkutsk. As they approached the time of the trains' departure, they made a big point of interacting with the troops as they shunted the carriages into place, sometimes giving them packets of cheap *Mahorka* tobacco, a rare bit of comfort for them since the Tzar had banned the sale of alcohol in Russia ahead of the First World War.

When the time came to connect the carriages containing the gold to the waiting locomotives the troops were indifferent to their actions. They coupled the armoured goods carriages containing the gold together and used their locomotive to shunt them into a turning "Wye" in the middle of the yard, out of sight of the troops.

The Wye enabled the railway equivalent of a three-point turn and allowed a train to quickly reverse its direction. But Dimitri and Sergei weren't just changing direction, they were swapping carriages.

They halted alongside the empty cargo carriages and jumped down from the locomotive's cab.

In a matter of moments, they had opened the leading gold carriage and transferred a crate of gold bars and a barrel of gold coins into the last of the empty armoured carriages.

Once both carriages were closed again, they swapped the identifying plates. Now all they had to do was shunt the carriages from train "D" into a siding, and replace them with the empty carriages attached to their locomotive before shunting them back down. They would then become part of Admiral Kolchak's official train convoy to Irkutsk.

CHAPTER FOURTEEN

Sergei and Dimitri had spent many years travelling the Trans-Siberian railway between Moscow and Vladivostok. They knew every station, branch line, spur, siding and marshalling yard, the best times to travel, the gradients and dangerous bends, and the speed they could be safely navigated at. Once Kolchak's train set off, it would be surrounded by chaos, and guarded by carriages packed with troops to protect the precious cargo. But that wouldn't trouble them now, because as night fell their five carriages and the locomotives at the front and the back of their train would slip away on a spur, looping round to the trans-Siberian mainline before beginning their long journey to Irkutsk.

CHAPTER FIFTEEN

The theft of the gold and the distraction caused by their orchestrated crash at Tatarskaya station were the first two steps of their plan. The next step involved the steep bend that curved around Lake Baikal. Dimitri pulled the brass regulator lever and heard the furnace roar as the air and fuel built up pressure in the boiler. The needle on the dial climbed towards its maximum of 200 psi, and he could delay the moment no longer. He took an oily rag and wiped the levers and dials. He released the brakes and felt the pistons shudder beneath his feet. The white feather of steam puffed out from the safety valve for the last time as he jumped down onto the frozen earth beside the track. The locomotive picked up speed as it headed down the hill towards the bend. The last of the carriages disappeared from view and only the fading clatter from the steel wheels carried through the freezing night air. He began to scramble down the precipitous embankment to where Sergei and the last ice-boat awaited. He was halfway down when he heard a gut-wrenching crash and the sound of splintering ice, as the locomotive and carriages concertinaed through the surface of the frozen lake below.

CHAPTER SIXTEEN

THE GROENING MUSEUM - PRESENT DAY

'That's genius! Katja said. 'Everybody's looking for the missing gold in the lake while it's headed for the Russian coast.'

'So how much of this can be proved?' Hoog asked.

Erika tapped a picture showing a newspaper article with a black and white picture of some locomotive wheels underneath the water.

'The Three Dimensions Diving Club discovered parts of a railway carriage at the bottom of Lake Baikal in 2011. According to the divers, it looked like the train was travelling way too fast into a bend, derailed, and toppled down the hillside into the lake.'

'So, until anybody finds any actual gold in Lake Baikal, we don't know if the story of the Kolchak gold train theft holds water...pun intended,' Katja said.

Erika pointed to an old newspaper cutting detailing a collision at Tatarskaya station. 'The crash at the railway station is well documented, though they never found out why it happened.'

A young woman in her twenties with an explosion of blonde tresses came over to Erika. She carried a tray with mugs of coffee and a plate piled high with biscuits. Erika introduced her.

'This is Hanna Krause,' Erika said. 'My new assistant. I'm getting too old to be lifting some of the heavy stock around, so she helps me with the larger items.' She indicated the detectives. 'Detectives Jochum Hoog and Katja Blondell. Ward you've already met; he's the more digitally aware member of our team.'

Hanna put the tray down and shook hands. Ward's told me a lot about your exploits,' Hanna said, giving them a broad smile.

'I'm sure,' Katja said.

'It's surprising how many young men have offered to help me organise my storage since Hanna started to work here,' Erika said.

'I wonder why,' Katja said with a smile.

'She's not just the brawn of the outfit though. She has a lot of knowledge and theories of her own when it comes to the incredible shrinking gold of the Romanov dynasty.'

Hoog bit into a biscuit. 'Mmmm.'

'Did I mention that she bakes her own biscuits,' Erika said. Hanna handed her a small container with some pills in it.

'You've just made a friend for life,' Katja said, looking at Hoog as he wolfed down another biscuit.

Erika swallowed her pills with a swig of coffee. 'I'm sure,' she said.

Hanna smiled and pointed at the biscuits. 'Plenty more where that came from.'

'So, what can you tell us that we don't already know?' Katja asked Hanna.

'My great grandfather was a U-boat captain in WW1 and my grandfather served on one in WW2 . So, with what they all passed down through the family I have a lot of stories.' Katja looked at the corkboard crowded with printouts of old Russian maps, locomotives and German submarines. 'So, if we're to believe that these engineers carried out the theft of the Romanov fortune from Kolchak's gold train, what happened to it next?' Erika moved nearer the corkboard and nodded at Hanna to speak.

'What I've been able to find out is based solely on the stories and hearsay passed down by my family. At some point the myth and the facts may well collide. Though at the moment it's just historical speculation.'

'Go on,' Katja said.

Hanna smiled. 'Erika knows a lot of this already, but let's assume you're not all as well versed in German and Russian history as she is.'

'That would be a very good assumption to make,' Hoog said.

'Okay. As the end of 1918 approached, it was obvious that the Germans were going to lose the war. Obvious to everyone except the German high command it seemed, as they were hell-bent on launching an all-out naval attack on the British fleet. This didn't go down too well with the public who were starving in the streets, or with the sailors who were being ordered to mount a battle they would almost certainly lose.'

Katja nodded. 'There was a revolt by the sailors of the German high seas fleet...'

Hanna took a sip of coffee before replying. 'Yes. The Keil Mutiny, during which they formed workers and soldier's councils modelled after the soviets of the Russian revolution. It was a revolution that would lead to the end of the German Empire and the establishment of the Weimar Republic. We don't need to know all of the details, but suffice to say that both Germany and Russia were in chaos.' Hanna paused. 'Don't worry, that's the end of the boring part.'

Erika shook her head. 'History's never boring. Go on.'

'Okay, now I'm relying on the stories passed down from my great grandfather, so suspend your disbelief until we have all the facts. Prior to the theft of the gold, two members of the *Moon Wolve*s, a driver and his engineer, travelled to Bruges...'

Hanna looked at her audience.

'If you're wondering, yes, I think these could be the same engineer and driver from the *Moon Wolves* that Erika told you about. The ones that would allegedly go on to steal Kolchak's gold.'

'Carry on.' Erika said.

'Okay. They tracked down a U-boat captain named Helmut Schroder. They managed to convince him that it would be better to leave the scene ahead of Germany's capitulation and put his U-boat to better use...I also imagine there was a monetary incentive.'

'They wanted him to transport the Romanov fortune out of Russia,' Katja said.

'Exactly,' Hanna said, 'they told him about the *Moon Wolves* organisation and their plan to steal the gold. All he had to do was lie low until the inevitable happened.'

'The fall of the Romanov Empire,' Hoog said.

'Yes. Once they learned of Kolchak's plans to steal the Romanov gold they would be in a position to intercept it while it was in the railway system, and orchestrate its transportation out of Russia.'

Ward looked up from his screen. 'So where did they

stash the U-boat between the war ending, and the theft from Kolchak's gold train?'

'Have you heard of Heligoland?' Hanna asked.

CHAPTER SEVENTEEN

UDA BAY, SIBERIA, 1918

The *Deutschland* sat waiting in Uda Bay on the Okhotsk Coast in Siberia. The bay had once been home to a whaling station, but now lay abandoned, its derelict buildings like pale rotting teeth in the polar night. They'd anchored off shore, and submerged down to periscope depth while they waited for the convoy carrying the gold to arrive. In the days of eternal twilight, the trucks would be able to unload their cargos with little danger of being spotted.

Captain Helmut Schroder put his face to the Zeiss eyepieces of the periscope and scanned the desolate landscape. In the distance he could make out the snow-covered ring of the Kondyor Massif Mountain.

Russia's vast landmass was in stark contrast to the

small island he and his crew had taken refuge in before Germany surrendered to the allies. Heligoland was just over one and a half square kilometres of archipelago in the North Sea, forty-six kilometres off the coast of Germany. With its battery of twelve-inch guns, rocky coastline and commanding view, Heligoland made an ideal fortress to protect the shipping route across the North Sea.

Heligoland was given up by the British to Germany in 1890 in exchange for Zanzibar, and under the German empire became a major naval base during the first world war. Helmut and some of his crew had grown up on Heligoland, and as children, had explored every nook and cranny on the island.

They'd marvelled at the natural phenomenon of Tall Annie, a 47-metre red rock column towering into the sky, and scrambled into the natural tunnels and rock faults around the coastline. They'd discovered the rock caves that were only accessible at low tide, and how to reach them through hidden passageways from the top of the cliffs. He remembered the exact moment he had decided to join the Navy.

He'd been lying on the grass at the cliff edge, looking out across the harbour. He'd crept out of the house with his father's powerful Zeiss binoculars, and watched, fascinated, as SMS *Heligoland*, a dreadnought class battleship of the Imperial German Navy, along with the rest of the High Seas Fleet, had arrived on a training exercise at the island's harbour. With a water depth of 47 metres, the harbour could easily accommodate the largest of battleships in the fleet.

Once Helmut and his crew had made the decision to leave Zeebrugge, they ensured the batteries were fully charged and the sub was fuelled. Under cover of darkness they headed out into the North Sea and set course for Heligoland.

Travelling only at night, it took nearly a week to reach the west of the island and navigate into the cavernous rock cave beneath the cliff.

It had been a nerve-racking journey, with an unknown number of mines still off the coast to be avoided, as well as any ships from either side. They didn't want to risk an encounter with a British warship, or have to explain their presence to the German authorities.

They submerged to periscope depth and edged below the archway of rock leading into the sea cave before opening the hatches. Helmut swung the boat's powerful searchlight around the dark interior.

The cave stretched 150 metres beneath the cliff before coming to a shallow sandy beach. He remembered bringing a girl down through the narrow entrance tunnel for a midnight feast, and a chance to satisfy his teenage hormonal needs. But that was another world, and back then Heligoland was a different place.

They tied off the U-boat using one of the rough spires of rock that jutted out from the water throughout the cavern, and adjusted her ballast to ensure she didn't float when the tide came in. Once night fell they could leave through the concealed entrance at the cliff-top. As long as they checked on the condition of the batteries and ran the diesel motors once a month the boat would remain serviceable. The British would be fully occupied destroying German armaments on the mainland, and have no reason to search for a U-boat they didn't even know existed.

Helmut's involvement with an anti-Russian resistance group had led him to where he was today. Thousands of miles from his home, in the dark days of winter, waiting to load his U-boat with a fortune in Romanov treasure. And as he waited, his mind went back to that first meeting with Sergei and Dimitri, months earlier.

They'd sat in *Le Trappiste*, a crowded, seventh century beer cellar near the Grote Market on Kuipersstraat, each nursing a glass of Brugse Zot, a local beer from the De Halve Man brewery in Walplein. *Le Trappiste* was a popular haunt for crews of the ships and U-Boats based in Zeebrugge. Helmut, initially wary at being approached by two burly Russians, was starting to relax. He took a sip of the strong beer from his glass and looked at Sergei quizzically.

'How are you able to travel so freely across borders and amongst all the different factions?' Helmut asked. Sergei smiled.

'That's a good question comrade, and it deserves a good answer. But first, for a sense of clarity I must ask you a question.' He took a mouthful of beer before continuing. 'In times of war, starvation and destruction, what is the one thing that can make the difference between success and failure?' Helmut thought about this for a moment. Throughout the war his mission had been to not only attack allied warships but to destroy ships supplying the enemy with food and arms. He didn't have to think for long, or search too hard for the answer.

'Supplies,' he said.

'Exactly comrade. And the main source of supply across the land is through the railway networks. You can't just jump into a locomotive cab and drive it to where you like. It's a skilled occupation. Imprisoning or killing a train driver would be like shooting yourself in the foot.'

'In both feet,' Dimitri interjected with a smile.

'Yes,' Sergei took a sip of beer.

Helmut nodded. 'So, everybody needs an engineer and a driver.'

'Yes. Wars end, alliances falter and leaders are deposed. But the world still needs to get food and arms to those that need them.'

'So, now we have established your importance, and how unimportant I am soon to be, what is the point of our meeting?' Helmut asked. Sergei fastened his gold-flecked eyes on him, gripping his shoulder with a strong hand before speaking. 'The point, dear comrade, is that we can be of great service to each other in these dangerous times. Helmut drained his beer glass and put it down.

'Okay, I'm listening.'

'Well, as you know we have had our own revolutions and uprisings, and we find ourselves at a point in history when empires will fall, taking their emperors down with them.' Helmut nodded.

'You're talking about the Romanovs?'

'Yes. When the Romanov empire falls, as it surely will, the vultures circling overhead will descend on their treasure and gold. And it doesn't matter where, or who it ends up with, at some point it will have to be moved.' He smiled, his teeth flashing white in the dim lights of the beer cellar. Satisfied Helmut was listening, he went on.

'And the only way to move hundreds of tons of gold over large distances in safety...is by train.' Helmut thought about this. It made sense. 'What's your plan?' he asked, casting a look around the room to ensure they weren't overheard.Sergei leaned nearer. 'We're members of a group of Russian dissidents known as the *Moon Wolves*. Our mission is to rebuild the German empire once the war is over, and make it great again.'

'For which you need money to buy arms, restore the country and rebuild their industries,' Helmut said. Sergei nodded.

'Exactly. Many of our members are engineers and drivers on the Trans-Siberian railway. It takes time and planning to load large amounts of gold into carriages. We'll have plenty of warning before they start to transport anything, anywhere. Once we have the gold, we need to get it to the coast.' Sergei waited for his response. Helmut's intuition had been correct. They had sought him out for a reason.

'You need to transport the gold by sea...or rather under it.'

'Precisely.' Sergei said, clapping him on the shoulder.

'The war is as good as over. If you get your submarine and your men to safety before it all falls apart, you will be helping us, and doing your crew a favour, a favour for which you will be well rewarded.'

Sergei watched the captain carefully for his reaction. Helmut took a sip of his beer. There was no denying that the war would soon be over. The signs were there for all to see. Only the deluded generals in High Command refused to accept the inevitable and were prepared to sacrifice thousands of soldiers and mariners to save face. He was being offered a chance to save the lives of his men and rebuild the German Empire, not to mention a substantial payment. It didn't take him long to come to a decision.'Very well, I'll ask my men, and they will probably follow my lead. No one wants to lose a boat to the allies,' he paused. 'How will you contact me with your instructions?'

'I can tell you your destination now, and all you have to do is await your code word and the date you need to be there.' Sergei paused. 'Do you have a name we could use as your code word?' he asked.

'*Forseti,*' Helmut said.

Sergei looked at him. 'I don't think we have any members of our group using that name. What does it mean?'

'It's a Norse god, part of the mythology of Heligoland where I was born.' Helmut said.

Sergei smiled. 'Okay. We'll contact you when we have a rendezvous date. You'll need to reach your destination early, and remain hidden until the trucks arrive.'

Dimitri drained his beer and banged the glass down. 'Another drink to the future, my friend!'

CHAPTER EIGHTEEN

The convoy had taken a tortuous route through the desolate landscape of Siberia, journeying for over a month in the perpetual darkness of polar nights.

The gold ingots were unloaded from the trucks and painstakingly transferred into the cargo hold, using a human chain. The submarine was over 90 metres long and principally a submersible freighter. With a range of 46,000 kilometres and a top speed of 12 knots, it could accommodate over 700 tons of cargo in its hold.

But even that wasn't enough. Every available space in the sub had been filled with the heavy gold bars. The battery compartment was already full and they'd been forced to stack more bars under bunks and unused compartments throughout the vessel.

The engineer studied the inclinometer and shook his

head. 'We need to store more cargo in the aft compartments or we'll never get her balanced.'

Captain Schroder agreed. With tons of gold stashed throughout the sub they would have the trim attributes of a drunken whale.

Their journey home would last months, taking them across the sea of Okhotsk, to the North Pacific Ocean, through the Bering Sea, into the Bering Strait and across the Arctic Ocean into the Barents Sea, before they finally reached the North Sea. It was a long enough journey in normal circumstances, and unless they could control the submarine's trim it would be impossible to complete their mission.

'Is there anything else we can do to balance ourselves?' Helmut asked.

The engineer shrugged. 'We may have to move the crew to the bow when we dive and aft when we surface,' he smiled. 'Or you could throw some gold into the sea.'

'Too many people have risked their lives helping us for me to justify that action,' Helmut said.

The engineer smiled. 'I was only joking, there's no way I would throw away all the work and courage shown by the *Moon Wolves*.' The engineer looked at the inclinometer again. It was showing 5% of down bubble.

He remembered back to the practice of having a Trim Party for any new officers of the deck when he had first joined as a submariner. Crew members would run to the front of the sub and cause the boat to down bubble. The officer would correct it, and then the crew would run to the back of the boat causing it to tilt up. After the third or fourth time the new officer of the deck would realise what was going on and stop reacting. The engineer smiled at the memory. There were few laughs to be had on board a wartime U-boat and that wasn't going to change anytime soon. The engineer shook his head.

'We'll just have to reorganise the storage of the gold until we get her level. I'll break it to the men.'

It was midday, and a dull red glow tinged the snow-capped mountains pink. In the depths of winter, the sun never rose above the horizon, and the area experienced a forty-day polar night with an eerie few hours of twilight at midday. With the last of the precious cargo loaded, the submarine slid beneath the surface.

As he looked through the periscope Helmut saw the exhausted faces of the men who had toiled through the night repacking the gold. They stared out across the bay at the foaming water thrown up by his submerging U-boat. He had handed out a crate of gold roubles to the train driver and his engineer to distribute to the men who had transported the gold across the lake, and carried out the loading operation. He hoped they would be able to start a new life wherever they chose to settle.

He swung the periscope round and looked out to sea from the inlet. They would have to dive beneath the ice floes that littered the sea at that time of year. It was a route that ships avoided because of the Arctic conditions, and for that reason was the safest route for them to avoid detection. He looked at the tired faces of his crew. They were starting a journey of almost three and a half thousand kilometres through enemy waters that were still patrolled even though the war was over. It would need all his skill and luck if they were to reach their destination safely.

Helmut turned to his second in command. 'How much Schnapps do we have left?'

The man smiled. 'Enough for a couple of rounds, Captain.'

Helmut smiled grimly. 'Get it all out. It's going to be a long trip.'

CHAPTER NINETEEN

THE GROENING MUSEUM, PRESENT DAY

Hanna paused. 'That's about as much as I've been able to piece together, and even then, it's only memories of my grandfather's stories mixed in with my great grandfather's, handed down through the years. I've researched as much as I can and filled in any holes with other accounts from WW1 submariners,' she paused. 'As you know, the wreck of a submarine was discovered last year off the coast of Oostende, and there's a chance that it could be our missing U-boat. It was declared a war grave, so there hasn't been any internal exploration of the wreck or its cargo.'

'Don't they all have an identification number?' Katja asked.

'Yes, but after a hundred years on the bottom of the sea the exterior markings are either gone or covered with rust and marine growth. But from what I can remember, she was identified by a marking on the propeller. Ward's been checking to see if those details were put online after the most recent dive,' Hanna said.

Wards looked up from the screen before speaking.

'Yes, it's taken a while to get the images I wanted you to see downloaded, the museum's servers aren't exactly state of the art.' Erika smiled. 'Cheeky,' she said. Ward shot her a smile before speaking.

'U-155, initially known as *Deutschland*. It was claimed as a kill by HMS *Landrail*. They sighted it in the Barents Sea, off the coast of Sweden. It was on the surface and attempting to dive when they engaged with it. They rammed it and dropped depth charges into the water where it had submerged. They saw underwater explosions beneath the surface and an oil slick after the attack. Naturally, they claimed it as a kill.' Ward looked up from his screen.

'It's been on the hydrographic charts since 1947, but in the 1980's it was initially recorded as a landing craft 25 metres down, and twenty kilometres off the coast of Oostende. Nowadays they have multi-beam echo sounders and sonar devices used for hydrographic surveys, which are far more sensitive than the technology used back then. When they scanned it again recently, they realised it wasn't a landing craft. It was shaped like a cigar, with pointed ends and a tower in the middle. It was obviously a submarine,' he tapped the computer tracker pad.

'I'm using the raw video data from the latest scan and a cool bit of software called *'Sea Thru'*

'What does that do?' Katja asked.

'It's a computer vision algorithm that lets us see what an underwater scene would look like if it was filmed through air instead of water.'

Ward said.

'How does it do that?' Hanna asked. Ward smiled.

'It gets pretty technical, so I'll give you the short answer. You can watch it working as I talk.' The monitor screen filled with a murky picture beneath the sea, and a dark shadow approaching the camera.

'Okay. *Sea Thru* removes the visual distortion caused by light travelling through the water to produce a colour accurate image. The program analyses the physics of light absorption and scattering in the atmosphere and compares it with the ocean, where the particles that light interacts with are much larger.'

'I'm glad this is the short answer.' Katja said, dunking a biscuit into her coffee. Ward smiled and went on.

'Nearly done. So then the algorithm reverses the image distortion from the water, pixel by pixel to show you an accurate restoration of the missing colours... look.' Ward pointed at the screen and they all looked towards the large monitor as he activated the program.

The murky colours of the sea began to gradually fade away and the dark shape of the U-boat began to take shape as the camera moved nearer. The colours of the marine life blooming across its hull shifted from dark green and blue to their real and much brighter colours.

'Wow, that's amazing,' Hanna said

The image on the screen now revealed the sunken U-boat in staggering detail...as if someone had pulled the plug on the ocean, letting it drain away to reveal the sub sitting on a bed of sand.

Ward nodded. 'Yes, it's pretty cool and you can see that when this was filmed there was no evidence of any damage to the outer hull. But it has sustained damage to its periscopes and conning tower.' Katja shook her head and looked at Hanna before speaking.

'If the *Landrail's* log confirmed the kill as being off the coast of Sweden, how did it end up 500 kilometres off course from Heligoland? 'I have some theories,' Hanna said.'Go on,' Erika said.

'Back in 1919, they didn't have the navigational equipment we take for granted these days. Submarines spent most of the time travelling on the surface, or at periscope depth.'

Erika nodded. 'Yes, they weren't that sophisticated back then, which is why so many of them were spotted on the surface and sunk.' 'That's for sure,' Hanna said, before going on.

'They relied on triangulated visual fixes, celestial and dead reckoning. I have some thoughts on how they managed to survive the *Landrail's* attack. I think the destroyer inflicted catastrophic damage. And that's what eventually killed them.' The team sat silently, until Katja spoke softly, 'So what do you think happened?'

CHAPTER TWENTY

BERENTS SEA - DEC 13th 1919

Kapitanleutnant Helmut Schroeder ordered his men to the torpedo room. If they were to pull out of their dive and get back to the surface, they needed to fool the destroyer above them. If the warship thought they were still alive it would be waiting for them when they surfaced, and that would be the end of them.

The torpedo lieutenant opened the number one torpedo hatch and began to stuff it with old rags and debris before sealing it and preparing to fire. The red warning light blinked on. The crew turned the wheels that opened the external doors of the torpedo tube and heard the rush of seawater as it surged into the hollow cylinder.

'First tube fire!'

The torpedo lieutenant pressed the firing button with his thumb and the U-boat shuddered slightly as the debris shot out into the ocean.

'Fire fuel ballast!' The engineer's crew worked the pressure wheels, pumping litres of fuel out from the ballast tank and sending it floating up to the surface. The captain looked at the depth gauge as the needle swung down. 30-40-50-60. He needed to get the boat back on trim or they would never pull out of the dive.

'Trim Party! All crew make your way to the storage areas, grab a gold bar and head to the bow.' The men hurried to obey, and soon a long line of men was shuffling down sixty metres of narrow gangway, crowding into the submarine's bow area, each clutching a fortune in gold.

The down bubble on the inclinometer began to move up. 25%-20%-15%-10%...the watch officer adjusted the tilt of the hydroplanes and gradually the bow began to level.

'Main engines full power!'

The hum of the electric motors throbbed through the boat as the U-boat's propellers clawed the water, fighting against its deadly descent. The depth gauge was now reading over 150 metres. The crew could hear the groaning of the hull as the pressure climbed inexorably with each metre they sank below the surface.

The crew stared at the captain, their faces pale and frightened, looking for some kind of miracle. Helmut wracked his brain for a solution. They'd shifted the cargo, vented the fuel ballast and were already at full power. Then it came to him. The torpedoes! The U-boat had three torpedo tubes and eighteen torpedoes. That was nearly thirty tons dragging them down.

'Torpedo Lieutenant, load and fire all torpedoes as fast as possible!'

The torpedo crew snapped into action, manhandling the torpedoes into the empty tubes and blowing the first tube clear of water. They turned the wheels that opened the external doors and the seawater rushed into the remaining two tubes. The lieutenant pressed the firing button with his thumb.

'First tube fire!'

'Second tube fire!'

'Third tube fire!'

The torpedoes hissed away.

'Close external doors!' The men rushed to seal the torpedo tubes' external doors and clear the empty cylinders of seawater before reloading the torpedoes and repeating their actions. Three at a time, the torpedoes were sent speeding out into the ocean. The men stood silently while the captain stared at the inclinometer bubbles and the depth gauge. Metre by metre the U-boat began to right itself. The down bubble worked its way back up...10%-5% until it was at zero. 'All trim secured, running level.' The dive officer snapped out. The men's faces reflected their hope as gradually the boat rose towards the surface.

'Up periscope.' Helmut raised the brass handles on the attack periscope. It moved up a few inches before jamming. Helmut wrestled with it for a moment and then moved to the secondary observational periscope. This one moved a little further, and then also jammed. Between the two views he could only see a sliver of the outside world.

'Slow surface,' Helmut said, and headed for the small ladder in the conning tower leading up to the bridge. He waited until the submarine had stopped moving and released the hatch. He heaved it up until it slammed against an obstruction. He managed to force it open a few more inches before it came to a halt. He peered through the narrow slit. What he saw confirmed his worst fears. The destroyer had smashed across the conning tower, destroying both periscopes, and the two deck guns. The periscopes had been bent over at right angles, and were preventing the hatch from opening.

They would have to make a journey of nearly three thousand kilometres along the coast of Sweden to reach the safety of Heligoland, virtually blind, without torpedoes or a functioning deck gun. He slammed the conning tower hatch shut and dogged the handles to secure it. He climbed down the narrow ladder, and with a heavy heart prepared to break the news to his waiting crew.

CHAPTER TWENTY-ONE

GROENING MUSEUM, PRESENT DAY

They sat silently for a moment, trying to imagine the gruelling journey the U-boat captain and his crew had made, before meeting their fate.

Hanna spoke first, 'It's a miracle they made it so far, considering how badly damaged they were. The initial dive on the wreck didn't conclude why the U-boat sank; their best guess was that they snagged the cable of an underwater mine with their damaged periscopes and it exploded, blowing a hole in their hull.'

'So, we still don't know for sure if this submarine is the source of the Romanov gold?' Katja said.

'Technically it's a war grave, so the divers were only allowed limited access to the wreck. Without a more intensive exploration on site it's impossible to know,' Ward said.

'Unless we make some headway with our badly dressed friends,' Hoog said.

'I did find something interesting,' Ward tapped the keyboard. 'I managed to get access to the CCTV data from the Oostende port authorities. I was able to get night footage from the last two years, and I also downloaded some footage from an Oostende beach webcam, but the visibility was pretty poor. It's taken a while to filter out the regular traffic and come up with anything abnormal in the shipping lane above the wreck. As you can imagine, it's as busy as a motorway with 200 metre tankers and cruise ships appearing every 15 minutes or so, but then I found this.'

The screen filled with footage of a cruise ship taking avoiding action to miss a dredger outside of Oostende harbour. Ward paused the clip.

'Then I did a search on YouTube for any videos taken around the same time, and came up with some mobile phone footage from the same night.' Ward ran a video clip which showed a passenger's eye view from the deck of the cruise ship as it avoided the same dredger.

Ward paused the feed.

'From the CCTV footage and the port authority records it seems the dredger was there for several hours during the night, apparently with engine problems.' Hoog studied the frozen frame on the computer screen.

'If there was gold in the submarine, would it be theoretically possible to dredge the gold up from that depth? Ward nodded. 'For sure. A trailing suction hopper would be able to suck up individual ingots and pump them into the hold of the dredger as long as they were accessible.'

Hoog scratched his chin. 'Bakker was a commercial diver. It wouldn't be too difficult for him to cut a hole in the side of the wreck to allow the dredger access.'

Katja looked at the screen. 'Do we know who owns the dredger?'

Ward zoomed in on the bow of the dredger. *Краб.* Ward did a quick Google search. 'It's Russian for crab.'

Erika smiled as she watched the toing and froing between the detectives. She leaned forward. 'If Bakker was tasked with making sure the dredger had access to the gold, he may well have scooped up a few ingots for himself. It was just unlucky that he got himself arrested while he was in possession of one.'

'If that's the case, and he was hired to dive the wreck, he must know where the rest of the gold is,' Katja said. 'Not necessarily, if it was loaded onto the dredger it could be anywhere by now.' Hoog said.

Erika shook her head. 'I don't think it was headed to another country. I think there's something else going on here.'

'Gold laundering?' Hoog asked.

'That's my best guess,' Erika said. 'You think it's still in Belgium and they're melting it down?' Hoog asked.'Yes,' Erika said, 'It's a way of turning gold into cash, provided the people with the gold could launder it on such an enormous scale.'

'What sort of people are we talking about?' Katja asked. 'Some years ago, I was dining with a rich Russian businessman...' Erika looked at their smiling faces. 'What? I used to have quite the social life, you know.'

Katja laughed, 'I don't doubt it. Go on.'

'Alright. Anyway, we were talking about the art world, and how perceptions of value come into play with things of beauty. And how gold has an intrinsic value, both politically and economically that affects the world's view, dependant on how much a country apparently holds in reserve. We discussed how it was impossible to know for sure how much gold a country really owned...until they were in desperate need and had to cash it in. The evening wore on, and we'd both had a fair amount to drink, when he leans over and says, '*Would you like to know a golden secret?*' Well of course I did.'

Katja smiled, 'You have us hooked. What did he say?'

Erika went on. 'He told me that there was a secret organisation that operated behind the scenes. An organisation that controlled the amount of gold in the financial system worldwide...'

'Rather like the way some people think that the diamond trade is rigged?' Katja said. 'The same.' Erika went on. 'He told me that it was in everybody's interest to keep gold scarce...'

'By everybody, I'm guessing he meant organised criminal gangs?' Erika smiled. 'Yes, a global operation involving organised criminal gangs, smugglers, art thieves...and governments. He told me the name of the organisation in Russian, but I'd drunk a lake of wine by then...'

'Any government in particular?' Hoog asked.

'No, but I got the impression it was at the very least the developed world...

'So, with all of the looting going on in war zones, and the many caches of Romanov gold and jewellery spread around, there's no shortage of customers for this mysterious Russian organisation,' Hoog said.

Ward looked up from the screen. 'It's highly unlikely that a petty thief like Bakker had the amount of money needed to buy a Romanov ingot on the black market. My bet is that he was involved in the operation to loot the sunken sub, and got a little light-fingered.'

Hoog nodded. The scope of their operation was spiralling out of control, and if he was being honest, he'd rather be joining Chandler, Duke and Roxie in Venice. The only way that was likely to happen was if they could prove Bakker's involvement with the gold and close the case quickly.

The Chief would probably read between the lines,

and want to avoid being drawn into a massive investigation involving law enforcement agencies around the world, especially as they had precious little evidence to go on.

He looked up and realised the rest of the team were looking at him.

'Sorry, I was just thinking how big this case could become if even half of what we think happened is a reality.'

Katja shared a look with him. 'It would take years of investigation, and if Erika's Russian friend was telling the truth, dealing with corrupt government officials and their involvement in the looting of war zones would make it virtually impossible to prove anything,'

Ward nodded. 'It would be a lifetime's work...with no way of knowing what the outcome would be.'

They looked at each other, their minds searching for a solution. Finally, Erika broke the silence. 'Ward's right. It's too big. Nobody's going to want to stir up an international hornet's nest of this magnitude. The best we can do is get enough information to pass the case on to the Feds and they can work with Interpol.'

Hoog rubbed his face. 'The Chief is not going to like this.'

CHAPTER TWENTY-TWO

Chief Nils Janssen leant back in his chair, the ancient wood and leather creaking in the quiet of his office. The chair was the only thing he'd brought with him when he'd been transferred from Antwerp into the post of Chief Commissioner in Bruges. The skeletal ergonomic carbon fibre monstrosity that greeted him had been consigned to another office. To hell with health and safety, Nils had a few rules that he lived his life by, and one of them was stick with what you know. And now, looking at the expectant faces of Hoog and his team, he was beginning to realise there was still a lot he didn't know. When he'd first arrived to take over the post of chief, he'd read their personnel records and especially that of Detective Hoog. There was no doubt he was a ferociously talented detective. Rescuing two female officers from a potential inferno and an agonising death, using a motorbike to climb the 306 steps of the city's ancient Belfort tower, had been a stroke of genius. The criminals behind the attack had assumed that no one could get to the top of the tower fast enough to save them, once the incendiary device had been tripped. ... luckily for the two women strapped to the bonfire, that wasn't the case.

Detectives Hoog and Katja, along with Ward and their international colleagues, had cracked a local drugs ring, shut down an organised criminal gang after a fire-fight beneath the city, and solved the mystery of a torso found in the canal, along with a dozen or more ancient corpses that threatened to disrupt the city's tourist trade.

They had served the force and the city well. The only thing outstanding was the priceless Holy Blood relic stolen from the Basilica during the confusion. The continued loss of the relic was a huge blow to the tourist industry, and getting Hoog and Katja off to Venice on the trail of the relic was his number one priority...but, that agenda was in jeopardy.

'So, what actual evidence do we have concerning the gold?' Nils asked.

He'd listened to their theories concerning the Romanov gold and its potential implications. The derailed train, the Russian *Moon Wolves* organisation and the sunken U-boat...but most of it was speculation.

Hoog spoke first. 'We can charge Bakker with theft, forging passports...' 'Driving with reckless abandonment on a scooter,' Katja added with a smile. 'Tho' that's not really what we'd like to pursue,' she said.

Nils held up his hand. 'Okay, the big picture is whether or not there is any more of this Romanov gold, if that's what it is. And, if so, how big an operation we would need to locate it. I'll be honest with you, I'm not looking to use up all of our resources on a hunt for the golden goose. I think we should charge them with what we've got, and if Bakker wants to do a deal to reduce his sentence and give us enough information to get Interpol involved, then so be it.'

It was what Hoog had hoped for; the Chief had no desire to get bogged down in a global investigation that could drag on for years. 'I agree Chief, we don't have the resources at local level.'

The chair creaked loudly as Nils got up. 'Okay, question him as soon as you like and charge him if he doesn't co-operate. And keep me in the loop' He picked up a newspaper with a lurid headline. 'I don't want to be reading about it in here first.'

Hoog headed towards the door. 'That's for sure Chief.'

CHAPTER TWENTY-THREE

They walked through the throngs of people at the Market, past the stalls and the ice rink teeming with children and parents tottering across the ice.'You know they're talking about moving the ice rink next year,' Ward said. 'Where to?' Katja asked. 'Minniwater. They're putting it on pontoons in the Lake of Love,' Ward replied. 'More cost cutting, I imagine,' Hoog said.'I think it's some kind of plan to spread the festivities more evenly around the city, rather than having it all concentrated into one or two areas,' Ward said. 'They're also cancelling the ice sculpture festival.' 'I heard it was to do with the need to go carbon neutral. The new ice rink will be made of plastic. The ice festival's cooling systems were consuming too much energy,' Katja said.

Hoog shook his head. 'There's going to a lot of

pissed off stall holders. The ice rink's a major tourist draw.'

He thought back to the ghoulish discovery of an ancient corpse beneath the ice rink during their earlier investigation and mused that it wouldn't have happened with a plastic rink.

'Another reason we need to get the relic back into the Basilica before people start to smell a rat. They're not going to believe it's being refurbished forever,' Katja said. 'That's for sure. I need a coffee,' Hoog said, ducking under a couple of tourists taking a selfie in front of the Jan Breydel and Pieter de Coninck statue, freedom fighters from the 14th century. It had been erected in 1887 when Romanticism was at its height in Europe and was always on the list of things tourists made a beeline for when they arrived in Bruges. They headed towards one of the many market stalls selling ice creams, snacks and coffees. 'I think Ward's taken a bit of a shine to Erika's new assistant,' Hoog said. Katja looked over at him. Ward's wife Mari had recently given birth to a baby boy, and along with his promotion to detective, Ward's life had suddenly become a lot busier. 'Really? I don't think so. It's just a bit of a midwife crisis. Having a baby doesn't exactly put the romance back into a relationship. Once they get a bit of sleep and organise a babysitter they'll be fine.''I suppose you're right. What are you having? Like I need to ask,' Hoog said.'Mochaccino and a waffle to go,' Katja said. They grabbed their coffees from a stall and headed into the Burg, cutting through Blind Donkey street and across the canal to the fish market. The market sold fish twice a week and jewellery, paintings, scarves and gloves for the tourists the rest of the time. Hoog watched a man operating a portable loom and marvelled at the dexterity that enabled him to produce a beautiful scarf one coloured strand at a time.

The man was from Eastern Europe and would spend a few months in Bruges over the holiday period, cashing in on the influx of tourists for his wares.'Do you think Bakker's got more ingots stashed away somewhere?' Ward asked.

Hoog took a sip of coffee. 'I don't know...' his mobile buzzed and he scooped it out of his pocket and studied the ID before tapping the screen. 'What's up Heidi?' Heidi worked in forensics for SICAD. Each judicial district had a communication and information service manned by federal and local police officers who gathered and shared intelligence to facilitate the co-ordination of investigations and day to day police operations.

Heidi was a willowy, intense woman with a laser-like focus on every case that came her way. Hoog could tell from her voice that she was excited about something. He listened, waiting until she'd finished speaking and he could get a word in. Heidi worked a couple of kilometres out of the city centre at the new police station in Lodewijk Coiseaukaai 3, an impressive glass and aluminium structure in the Sint Josef district opposite the Klein Handlesdok. 'Okay, we'll see you soon,' Hoog pocketed his mobile, 'That was Heidi.'

'She sounded excited,' Ward said. 'Yes, she's been checking out the gold ingots...' Hoog said.

Katja looked at him. 'And?'

Hoog smiled. 'All that glisters is not gold.' Katja continued his quote.

'Often have you heard that told.'

'I'm impressed,' Hoog said.

Katja smiled. 'So you should be. Many a fleeing crook has been stopped in his tracks by my witty Shakespearian repartee.' Hoog smiled, drained his coffee cup and they headed off.

CHAPTER TWENTY-FOUR

Police Station - Zeveneke

Within twenty minutes they were driving past the barrier and into the secure parking at the Zeveneke police station. Heidi was waiting for them in reception and they were soon travelling in the lift up to the top floor and her lab. 'Coffee?' she asked as she swiped her card through the entry lock. 'For sure,' Hoog said.

'Great,' Katja and Ward said as one. Heidi went over to a small coffee machine and busied herself preparing the drinks. 'Thanks for coming over. I knew you would have a lot of questions, and showing you is quicker than you having to wait for my official report.' The coffee machine spat a dark gruel into their waiting mugs. Heidi swapped the cups over with consummate ease and they were soon sipping at their individual coffees.

She moved over to a glass cabinet with sliding doors. Inside were a large water filled graduated glass beaker, various metal implements, some small bottles of chemicals, and a gold ingot.

Heidi always made a point of explaining her processes whenever possible. Though it wasn't strictly necessary, she found detailing her analysis to the investigative team had cut down on any requests for forensic information based on unrealistic time frames. It always amused her to see TV shows where the detectives demanded DNA or physical analysis within half the time the beleaguered coroner had originally promised. It certainly didn't mirror her own experiences, and she was convinced her technique was partly responsible for that.

She looked around at the assembled Detectives before starting. 'Okay. The second gold ingot you found was authentic, so I checked the original one. First thing I did was a density test.' Heidi opened the glass cabinet and took the ingot out. She placed it on a weighing machine and noted the weight in grams. She then picked up the ingot, carefully lowered it into the water-filled glass beaker and noted the reading in millimeters.

She took the ingot out and placed it on the floor of the cabinet. She picked up a calculator and tapped some figures into it.

'We now have two readings. We deduct the second

reading from the initial measurement. Then we divide the gold's weight by the difference in the water level.'

Hoog smiled. 'The Archimedes Principle.'

'I think I skipped that at school,' Katja said.

Heidi went on. 'King Heiron II of Syracuse had a gold crown made and wanted to make sure its maker wasn't cheating him by mixing silver in with the gold...' 'Oh, wait a minute, wasn't Archimedes the guy that yelled Eureka, jumped out of his bath and ran naked through the streets?' Katja said.'I think that story was embellished; he probably did all his thinking in the bath,' Hoog said.

Heidi smiled. 'Hoog's partially right. Archimedes took one piece of gold equivalent in weight to the crown and one piece of silver of the same weight. He discovered that the gold displaced less water than the silver, so when he put the crown in the liquid it displaced more water than the gold. So, from that he deduced it must have been mixed with silver.'

Heidi looked at the calculator before continuing. 'The density of gold equals its mass divided by its volume. The standard density of gold is 19.3g/ml. If our reading is way off, then chances are we're looking at something that's not pure gold.'

Hoog leaned forward to look at the ingot. 'So, this is a fake?'

Heidi slipped some latex gloves on. 'A density test

doesn't always tell us if the item is pure gold even if the figures add up, as there are other materials that weigh roughly the same. Like Plutonium, Iridium Osmium and...'

Hoog started singing. 'Platinum, Rhenium and Neptunium...,' he stopped. 'What. You don't know that song?'

Heidi shook her head. 'You're very special aren't you,' she said

'Special needs more like,' Katja said.

Heidi smiled and went on.'There's also Tungsten, which I believe is what we may have here. Most of the other metals are too expensive or dangerous to work with.'

Heidi put the ingot into the cabinet, took a sharp implement and scratched the bottom of the ingot. She started an extractor fan and opened one of the chemical bottles...carefully using a glass eye dropper to drip the chemical onto the scratch. 'What's that?' Ward asked. 'Nitric acid.'

The chemical hissed on the surface of the ingot, turning it green where Heidi had made the scratch. She switched off the fan and wiped the ingot with a cloth before bringing it out of the cabinet. 'If the gold changes colour it's not pure gold. I think you'll find this is gold plated tungsten.'

'So how can we know if the second ingot we found is an authentic Romanov gold ingot?' Katja said.

Heidi placed the two gold bars side by side.

'Each bar has a unique serial number which can be verified. In this case it's easy to see that something's not right here.' Hoog and Katja looked closely at the bars.

'Because they both have the same serial numbers,' Katja said.

'Yes, and if you look closely you'll see they have the same mould marks.'

Heidi pointed at some distinctive scratches that matched each of the bars.

'So, the fake bar was made using a mould of the real Romanov ingot,' Hoog said.

'As far as we can tell, yes.' Heidi said. Hoog looked at the gold ingots.

'So, if Bakker used the original bar to make a mould and then used platinum and gold to make the fake...'

'Then he must have more gold stashed somewhere to coat the platinum,' Katja said.

CHAPTER TWENTY-FIVE

GROENINGE MUSEUM

They sat in the storage room beneath the Groeninge museum in their makeshift incident room staring at the photo printouts on the wall.

Hoog said, 'If Heidi's right he probably uses the real ingot to sucker people in, and then sells them a fake.'

Ward looked at a printout of the original ingot. 'He probably focuses on gullible tourists. After all, any legitimate dealers would know it was illegal to deal in Romanov gold, but if you spin a tourist some line about how you found the gold and want to get rid of it cheap, then you'll always find some mug to believe you.'

Katja paced around the small area.

'We still don't know how many real Romanov ingots are involved. Bakker could be using gold from another source to manufacture these fakes.''Gold is still over a thousand euros an ounce, and even using titanium coated with gold the ingot would cost over forty thousand euros,' Ward said. 'Well, considering the real deal is worth over 400,000 euros that's a good profit, even if he sold it at half price,' Hoog said, scratching an ear. 'I'd say that he could have got his hands on some of the real ingots while salvaging the motherlode from the U-boat for his masters.' 'I think there could be another possibility,' Ward said. 'Go on,' Hoog said.'Maybe he was paid by this mysterious criminal gang leader in gold, and he's melting down the gold to make these fakes?' Katja said. 'That makes sense, even if he only got one, half a million euros is good pay for a night's work.' They mulled this over.

Hoog broke the silence. 'He could also have been paid with an ingot, and kept a few back for himself. After all, there's no real way of monitoring how many ingots were originally in the U-boat, if that's where they came from.' 'It reminds me of the pelicans and the gulls,' Katja said. She remembered long hot summers as a teenager at her grandma's home in Bradenton, Florida. Her grandma had left Bruges and bought a small unit overlooking the bay when she retired. In the early evenings Katja had sat watching the birds feeding as the setting sun threw a shard of golden light towards Sarasota on the far side of the bay. She'd been fascinated by the large and ungainly pelicans as they dive bombed the shoals of fish swarming beneath the surface. 'What about the pelicans?' Hoog asked.

Katja smiled. 'I used to watch them diving into the bay at my grandma's place in Florida. They'd scoop up a load of fish with their big beaks, and the second they surfaced a little gull would appear right next to them, waiting to grab any of the fish they dropped.'

Hoog nodded. 'Just like Bakker scooping up some gold ingots for himself while he hands over the bulk of the treasure trove to Mr big...whoever he is.'

Erika had been listening to them in silence, absorbing their theories and now she spoke,

'Whatever version is the truth, there's one thing that I believe applies to all of the possibilities.' Hoog nodded for her to go on.

'If Bakker stole ingots from the sunken U-boat without his boss knowing, he's going to be in big trouble if he's found out.' 'He's going to want to keep that quiet,' Katja said.

'And that gives us a lever,' Hoog said.

Katja looked at him. 'If his boss is heading up a gold laundering business and melting down gold bullion, he's going to need large scale industrial premises...or maybe he's paying or coercing a legitimate foundry into letting him use their facilities on the quiet.'

'I think it's time to have another little chat with Bakker,' Hoog said.

CHAPTER TWENTY-SIX

Kartuizerinnenstraat Police Station

Hoog pushed through the police stations' glass doors into reception. A bright-eyed man with a couple of days' stubble, and a small rucksac was leaning on the counter in front of Sophia De Vos, the officer at reception, as if he had all the time in the world. From the expression on Sophia's face it was obvious she didn't share his timescale.

Hoog flicked a look to Ward and Katja. 'I'll see you down there.'

Ward and Katja nodded and headed down the stairs leading to the interview rooms beneath the station.

Sophia was tall and lithe with dark, caramel eyes that missed nothing, and an ethereal air of calm. The image she projected had a lot to do with the black belt she held in Karate, and her proficiency in numerous other martial arts. Hoog had been happy to have her at his side during the odd drunken brawls he'd faced out on patrol back in the day.

The man in front of her was Kurt Van De Breen, known as CB, short for Conspiracy Breen. His ancestors were apparently Irish Franciscans who settled in the city of Leuven, east of Brussels, in the 1600's. Kurt would regale anybody who would listen about his ancestry. Originally from County Kilkenny, the former kingdom of Ossory in the province of Leinster, his family was descended through the Heremon line and claimed to be direct descendants of King Nial of the nine hostages, also known as the Lords of Brawney.

Over the years he'd become an all too familiar visitor to the police station. He was always alerting them to some new conspiracy and insisting it was a danger to the public. Sophia gave Hoog a despairing look. She had a ton of paperwork to do and Kurt wasn't helping at all. Kurt tapped the large ring on his finger intermittently against the glass, which further irritated her.

Hoog nodded to Kurt. 'Hi Kurt, what's happening in your world?' Sophia slid away, shooting Hoog a grateful look. Kurt produced an iPad from his rucksack and tapped open some pictures before speaking. 'Chemtrails, man. They're using aluminium now, you can see from the colour of the contrails.' Hoog sighed. He'd heard this conspiracy theory before. Kurt believed that the government was seeding jet fuel with chemicals as part of an operation known as SLAP, short for Secret Large-scale Atmospheric Program.

The followers of this theory alleged that the water condensation trails from aircraft contained chemical, biological agents, or a toxic mix of aluminium strontium and barium. The conspiracy theorists believed that SLAP was an operation run by the deep state to control the weather or to manage solar radiation. It was a theory that had never been proved, but that didn't stop Kurt from insisting it was true.

His belief in covert geo-engineering was unshakeable. Hoog had some sympathy with people that society judged as eccentrics, or crackpots.

After all, for many years nobody had given much credence to Greenpeace and their cause. They were seen as terrorists and their boat, *Rainbow Warrior*, had been blown up and sunk by the French intelligence in 1985.

Now with the desperate state of the world's climate and the burgeoning Extinction Rebellion movement, along with its worldwide support for Swedish climate activist Greta Thunberg, things had changed. Hoog studied the pictures on Kurt's iPad. They made no sense to him, but he was sure that Kurt found them deeply worrying.'Looks like you got some good pictures here. Why don't you email me a copy and I'll get a scientist friend of mine to take a look. Okay?'

Kurt nodded. 'Thanks man, I'll do that,' he leaned towards Hoog conspiratorially, dropping his voice. 'I'm working on something else at the moment. I can't tell you much, but I have some theories about your missing statues.' 'Good to know. By all means, get in contact if you think we can help, and thanks for dropping by,' Hoog said. 'No problem.' Kurt stowed his iPad in the rucksack, shifted it on his back and gave a wave as he left the station.

Sophia materialised next to Hoog. 'I don't know how you put up with him,' she said.

Hoog shrugged. 'Even a stopped clock is right twice a day.'

Sophia went behind the desk and shuffled some papers. 'Maybe, but do you believe any of the lunacy he's peddling?'

Hoog smiled at Sophia's frustration. 'People were probably saying that about Galileo when he tried to convince them about heliocentrism...' Hoog looked at Sophia's puzzled expression before going on. 'The belief that Earth and the planets revolve around the sun, rather than geocentrism which placed the Earth at the centre.'

Sophia shook her head. 'Of course, I knew that. As far as I remember that didn't sit well with the Roman inquisition.' 'That's for sure,' Hoog said.'You'll be telling me you believe the Earth is flat next.'

Hoog smiled. 'You'd be surprised at the number of people that have signed up for that one.'

Sophia snorted and leaned forwards. 'So how do they explain the thousands of pictures of Earth from the international space station?' 'Because obviously they're all photo-shopped,' Hoog said. 'Of course they are. Well, you're welcome to all the fruit and nutcases in that asylum,' Sophia muttered. 'I have enough lunatics to deal with on a daily basis. I find it amusing he has a replica CIA ring with their motto engraved on it.'

'The truth shall set you free," Hoog said. 'Yes,' he's probably a big fan of Mel Gibson in Conspiracy Theory.' 'He's harmless enough, and his ring's rather like that necklace you wear; it probably comforts him.' Sophia touched the silver St Christopher pendant hanging around her neck. It had once belonged to her mother and she was never without it. 'Maybe,' she said.' 'He's been useful in the past with a few investigations. He's almost certainly on the Asperger's scale, and people like that can see patterns in random incidents that we wouldn't notice.'

Sophia put her paperwork down.

'Okay, let's assume for one moment that I have nothing better to do than bury myself in conspiracy theories; what has he come up with that's helped you on a case?' Hoog thought for a moment.

'Well, many years ago we had a spate of bicycle thefts

from outside the station in Bruges, as well as in Ghent. We didn't have sophisticated facial recognition back then, and we were short staffed and up to our necks in day to day duties.' 'Go on,' Sophia said. 'Well, Kurt was just as eccentric back then but I used to tolerate him as I found him quite amusing...' 'You being a bit of a conspiracy geek yourself,' Sophia said.

Hoog gave a wry smile. 'Maybe. Anyway, one night, while I was working the late shift he came into the station with one of his conspiracy theories and I suggested he could focus on something a bit more down to earth.'

'Like bicycle thefts?' Sophia asked. 'Exactly. I sat him down in an interview room with a pile of CCTV footage, gave him a cup of coffee and left him to it.''What happened?' Sophia asked.

'Well, he was at it right through the night, staring at the footage and making notes, and by morning he'd cracked the case.' 'How?' Sophia asked. 'He'd managed to isolate a man who regularly went to work without a bike but took one from the rack on his way home.' 'How did that work?' Sophia asked.

'Well, sometimes he would take one from Bruges on his way home, and other times he would steal one from Ghent. He had a pair of very small bolt cutters so he was through the locks and off in seconds. Kurt was able to pick out this guy's face from all of the other students coming and going to and from the stations. Once we knew who to look for we just set up surveillance and caught him red handed.'

'I remember that now. He was a teaching assistant... you got all the credit for that arrest. No wonder you have a soft spot for Kurt.'

Hoog held his hands up. 'It's not as bad as it sounds. Kurt didn't want any of the credit for solving the crime. He was such a conspiracy nut back then he preferred to keep a low profile. So yes, I cut him some slack now and then.' 'Where does he live? He always looks a bit dishevelled; he's not sleeping rough, is he?''No. That's just Kurt, he likes to be invisible. He has a small room at the top of one of the Gentpoort towers, above the museum. They let him stay there in exchange for security and some cleaning work.''I guess he has a good view of the contrails from there,' Sophia said.'For sure,' Hoog said.'Maybe I should use him to clear up some of my backlog,' Sophia said.

Hoog smiled. 'It wouldn't harm your chances of promotion if you had another successful case under your belt when the next DI position comes up. Did you hear what he said about the missing statues?'

'Yes. But they're probably in a scrapyard somewhere in the Netherlands, or part of a brace of propellers on a boat in the Bosporus by now,' Sophia said.

Hoog shook his head. 'We don't know that for sure.

Maybe Kurt knows more than us.' Hoog looked at his watch. 'I have an interrogation waiting with our tight-lipped scooter friend.'

'Bakker? Seems like his case is growing faster than Pinocchio's nose,' Sophia said. 'Yes. We should be in Venice by now, but that won't happen until we put this case to bed,' Hoog said. Sophia shrugged.

'Far be it from me to say, but you might be better off out of it, given the flooding situation in Venice right now.'

Hoog nodded. 'I know, but I miss them. You know what it's like. Chandler, Duke and Roxie were part of our team.'

Sophia understood where he was coming from. She knew how strong the bond was between colleagues. They soon became family. Family you would die for. 'I hear you. Good luck with the interrogation, and I'll keep my fingers crossed the rest of your team stay safe.' Hoog smiled and headed towards the stairs leading to the interview rooms.

CHAPTER TWENTY-SEVEN

Katja and Ward sat waiting behind the two-way glass that looked through into the interview room. Bakker sat on one side of the table flanked by his lawyer. They weren't speaking and the lawyer occasionally looked down at his watch. It was obvious Bakker wasn't one of his favourite clients.

'So, how's fatherhood treating you?' Katja asked.

Ward smiled, and rubbed his eyes. 'A lot of noise and very little sleep.'

'I can imagine,' Katja said.

'It's amazing the things you take for granted: sleeping, going out...not cleaning up a smelly nappy.'

Katja nodded. She'd never been afflicted by a desire to have children, but knew at some point her hormones would try and hijack her. But right now, with her newly re-ignited relationship with Hoog, she was more than happy to miss out on a life of motherhood and smelly nappies. 'Rather you than me,' Katja said.'Mari's pretty good at keeping me away from the projectile vomiting, so I can't complain.'

Katja imagined how easily a household could get out of control with tired parents, baby food flying through the air and nappies piling up. She was too much of a control freak to embrace the chaos theory alongside the complexity of their ongoing investigations.

Though she welcomed the possibility of getting stuck into their ongoing case in Venice. She hadn't had any updates for a few days and was already missing the emails and occasional photos from Duke, Chandler and Roxie. She smiled at Ward.

'Mari's a great mother, you've got a winner there.' She looked at him. 'Have you heard anything from our friends in the land of the gondola?' Ward flipped open his laptop and checked his emails and media sites. 'Nothing recently. They might just be busy.'

'I suppose so,' Katja said.'You can't conduct door to door when the city's under two foot of water. It's complex enough navigating along the canals normally, without the streets being flooded as well.'

"You're right, it's not going to be easy. I just hope we can solve this case quickly and I get to join them,' Katja said. Ward looked across at Bakker and the lawyer.

'He doesn't look like he's in a hurry to spill the beans, does he?' Katja shook her head. He had a point. They were going to have to rely on Hoog's skills as an interrogator, or some kind of a breakthrough that led them to the rest of the gold.

The door behind them swung open and Hoog came in. 'Okay, let's try and get something useful out of our friend, shall we,' he said. 'Why not,' Katja said. Ward looked down at his computer screen. 'I think I'll stay here. I'm trying to access the network backup files from his mobile.' 'I didn't think we found his phone?' Katja said.'We didn't, but if I can get into his WhatsApp account I might be able to download files from the cloud.' 'Okay, that makes sense, and you are nearer the coffee and biscuits,' Katja said.'There is that,' Ward said. 'Do you want me to bring something in for you?'

Katja smiled.'No, we're fine, besides, my mother always used to say, be wary of geeks bearing gifts.' Ward shook his head as he watched them leave. 'Very funny. I'll ping you if I find anything.'

CHAPTER TWENTY-EIGHT

'No comment.' Bakker sat opposite Hoog and Katja in the interview room. His stonewalling had been going on for half an hour, and in his mind's eye Hoog imagined himself battering Bakker with a police truncheon. He leaned forward. 'Okay, here's the situation. No offence, but we're not really interested in you. It's nothing personal, but we have bigger fish to fry. We can charge you with theft, forgery, resisting arrest, and fraud.'

Bakker looked up. 'The gold was planted on me; how would I know if it was a fake?'

Hoog shrugged. 'So, somebody planted a fake gold bar in your pannier, and then we found the original it was copied from at your place of work. How do you explain that?' 'No comment,' Bakker said.

Hoog gathered some folders off the desk. 'It doesn't really matter, we just thought it was worth offering you the chance to mitigate the charges by telling us who you're working for.

Bakker shook his head. 'No comment.'

Hoog shrugged. 'Well, as I said, we don't really need you. Your friend is more than happy to give us the names we need and the location they operate from.'

Hoog looked for a reaction from Bakker and was happy to see the look on his face shift from blank indifference to worry. Bakker had nowhere to go on this. The one chance he had of reducing his sentence was slipping away. The thought of his accomplice getting off scot free wasn't something that sat well with him.

'I don't believe you,' Bakker said, staring unblinkingly at Hoog.

'Well, I guess that's something I'll have to live with. Once we've arrested the people behind the operation, your friend...' he looked down at a charge sheet. 'Finn... will be drinking wine in the sun, while you're locked up in Lantin.'

Bakker shrugged. 'Rats don't last long on the outside,' he said.

'Oh, I fully understand that. Honour amongst thieves. Eh? The problem is, the people you work for won't know which one of you two ratted them out,' Hoog said.'So?' Bakker replied. 'So, your friend Finn will be living in a nice safe house with a different identity somewhere warm, while you will be in a grubby little cell in prison, where, for a packet of cigarettes and some vodka someone could drastically alter your life expectancy.'

Bakker shook his head. 'You can't do that,' he said.

'You could get a bad judge on a bad day and be looking at maybe ten years? Forging police warrant cards and stealing passports along with the fake gold operation, it all adds up. And I'm guessing if we really went to town on your antique shop we could probably turn up all sorts of other things you didn't even know were there. What do you think?' Hoog waited. Bakker's lawyer wagged a finger at Hoog and gave him an admonishing look.'No way I'd get a ten-year sentence,' Bakker said, leaning back in his chair. 'Well as I said, it will all be pretty academic once you're in Lantin.' Bakker rubbed sweat from his forehead and said nothing. Hoog tried another approach.

'Let's talk about something different. You're a diver, we know that for sure. You're also in possession of what appears to be Romanov gold. I'm sure you're aware of the recent discovery of a sunken World War One U-boat off the coast of Oostende.'

Bakker shrugged. 'I read the papers.''Okay, well let's just suppose that these two facts are related, your ability to read, and the possibility that you were involved in illegally diving the site of a war grave. And let's go the extra mile and assume that you were operating with a dredger to facilitate removing a substantial amount of gold from the U-boat's hold. Now, if you were to admit to this, then you might only be charged with illegal trespass on a war grave and theft of archaeological artefacts.' Bakker thought about this. Hoog looked at Bakker's lawyer and gave him a verbal nudge.

'I'm no lawyer, but if you were to help us locate the gold from that submarine you might even be looking at a suspended sentence.' Bakker leaned over and whispered into his lawyer's ear. The lawyer shrugged. 'No comment,' Bakker said. There was a soft beep from Katja's iPad on the desk in front of her. She angled the screen towards Hoog and he read the text. 'We've got him.' File attached.

CHAPTER TWENTY-NINE

Ward looked around as Hanna entered the observation room and stood beside him. She'd heard Bakker's last statement. Ward tapped the screen and the laptop made a whooshing sound as a file shot off across the internet'So he's still playing hardball?' Hanna asked.

Ward smiled. 'Yes, but not for much longer. I managed to hack into the backup files in his WhatsApp account.''What did you find?' Hanna asked.'Well, he's denying everything as you know, even though he's a commercial diver. However, he couldn't resist videoing his last dive. What he didn't know is that WhatsApp automatically backs up all the files into the cloud.'

'Awesome, so this is the point when the suspect denies everything and the detective produces a piece of irrefutable evidence...I love it when that happens,' Hanna said.

'Me too...and you can see it in real time,' Ward said, tapping the screen.

Bakkers powerful headlamp lit up the massive hulk in front of him. Sixty-five metres long and ten metres high, its barnacle-encrusted conning tower and mangled periscopes loomed up out of the gloom. After a century on the seabed it had become an amorphous lump of corroded metal, swamped by marine growth.

He activated the camera on his mobile through the waterproof case and clipped it onto the side of his helmet. He swam towards the sunken U-boat and unclipped the laser template projector from his belt. He'd studied the internal blueprint of the *Deutschland*, a U-151 class submarine, and knew its layout in detail. But he needed to know exactly where to employ the thermal lance for maximum effect. The chances were that some of the ballast tanks contained unused fuel, or oil, not to mention the torpedoes that could still be on board and deadly. Along with the dangerous chemicals in the battery compartment it added up to a lot of hazards to steer clear of.

He set up the laser projector on a small tripod and

switched it on. He studied the rectangular template it had projected onto the side of the U-boat and adjusted it until he was happy. It would give him the precise guidelines to cut into the hull and gain access to the freight hold. He turned on the high-pressure gas feed, lit the thermal lance, and started work.

It didn't take long. A hundred years of corrosion made his job a lot easier, and he was soon making the final cut along the top of the hull into the storage space behind. The bubbles streaming from the cuts in the hull told him that the compartment had been sealed, and was now filling with water. He waited for the bubbles to stop and the pressure to equalize.

He used a small pry bar to force the metal plate away from the sub's hull. The heavy rectangle of metal tore free from the marine growth and tumbled to the seafloor. A gleaming avalanche of ingots cascaded through the cavity, forming an untidy mountain of gold in the mud beside the U-boat.

He switched over to his air tank and unhooked the umbilical. He didn't want to risk fouling his umbilical in the close confines of the U-boat. The air tank would give him 15mins of dive time at his present depth of 30metres. It wouldn't take long to check inside the U-boat in case there was a secondary storage area for the gold. He let himself drift down through the opening in the hull and into the void beneath. The light from his head torch revealed a floor littered with gold bullion.

It was going to be easy enough to guide the dredger's sucker into the compartment first, and then move it outside to pick up the gold strewn across the seabed.

He moved slowly over to the door at the back of the hold and pulled the heavy handle down to open it. The submarine was already flooded, so the door opened easily, and he floated through it into the darkness.

As he made his way down the narrow passageways it soon became obvious that apart from the freight hold the entire sub had been flooded. This was highly unusual.

When a sub was holed, it was standard operating procedure to seal all the watertight doors to contain the flooding. Even if this meant the loss of crew members trapped behind the doors. But as he moved through the eerie passageways it became obvious that something had happened to the crew of UB-151, and whatever it was had been catastrophic.

He swam slowly down the dark, steel passageways leading through the interior of the submarine. After resting on the seabed for a hundred years, silt had infiltrated into the very fabric of the boat, producing a swirling carpet of sand that eddied past his face mask as he slowly explored the rusty metal coffin it had become.

He passed skeleton after skeleton, some lying in their bunks, others upright at their posts. Whatever had gone on in the last death throes of the crew and the U-boat, it looked as if they had decided to remain at their posts. He wondered if they had simply drowned, or taken the easy way out with their Lugers. He let himself float to the floor of the companionway and felt something slide beneath his flipper. He looked down and saw more dull ingots of gold lying beneath the disturbed silt.

He slipped a few bars into some empty pouches around his waist. He couldn't take more on this trip without more buoyancy. Looking around in the gloom, he saw fish darting away from the glare of his torch and dozens of skeletal remains stretching into the dark.

He felt the sub vibrating under the pressure change, and then heard the distant sound of propellers approaching. He looked at his watch. It was past midnight. The dredger was already moving into position and he needed to be ready to guide the powerful sucker into the hold of the U-boat.

As he slowly drifted through the deserted steel

canyons, past the bleached bones of its crew, he felt as if the eye sockets were watching him as he passed. As if they had been waiting all those years, waiting for him to feel their pain.

Hoog and Katja sat silently as the video died and the screen went to black. They'd seen Bakker's face as he'd watched the video. It was pointless for him to deny his involvement.

'So, you helped yourself to a few gold bars while no one was looking?' Hoog said.

Bakker nodded, 'They owed me. Putting me through that shit.'

Hoog sat back in his chair. Bakker had obviously been terrified by what he'd seen. But he was also frightened of the people that had paid him to plunder the U-boat. Hoog needed to capitalise on that fear. He was a great believer in keeping things simple, and it didn't get any simpler than fear and greed.'Okay, well I think we've seen enough. We'll charge you with what we've got and release you on police bail. Bakker looked at Hoog. This wasn't something he'd seen coming. Katja smiled. She'd seen Hoog use this move before.'What?' Bakker said.

Hoog stood up, followed by Katja. Hoog paused on his way out. 'I just hope the press don't get hold of this.

You know how they blow things up out of all proportion.' He did some air quotes. 'Petty thief found with billions in Romanov gold.'

It didn't take more than a few seconds for Bakker to put the potential consequences together. 'But I don't have a fortune in gold,' he said.

Hoog leant down. 'As I say, the press always exaggerates things, and some people tend to overreact.' Bakker knew exactly what sort of people Hoog meant. The people he'd been working for. Hoog turned to go.

'Wait!' Bakker said. Hoog turned around to look at him. 'Something you want to share with us? 'Okay. I'll take you to where the operation is run from. In exchange, you set me up in a safe house with a fresh identity and a suspended sentence. Madeira's nice all year round, if you're asking.' 'Why not just tell us where the operation's being run from?' Hoog said.

Bakker shook his head. 'No, I don't want any leaks. If they find out their operation is compromised they'll disappear and I'll be a dead man.'

Hoog nodded. 'Okay, but if this is a waste of time, I'll make sure you get a trial with a bad judge on a bad day.'

CHAPTER THIRTY

Hoog gestured towards a sleek white car in the corner of the car park. 'We have a new arrival in the motor pool. A top of the range Tesla X. This baby can do things you wouldn't dream of.' He pulled out his mobile. 'Keys are a thing of the past.' He tapped the screen and the car reversed into the wall with a dull thud. 'Oops. Still getting to grips with the auto-summoning. Must have set the proximity too tight.' He tapped the screen again and the car crept towards them before halting in front of Hoog. 'That is creepy,' Katja said. 'But you know what I'm like with smartphones.'

Hoog smiled. 'How many is it now?'

'Quite a few, but it costs the department a lot less than your carpool write-offs.' 'Touchê.' Hoog produced a key fob from his pocket and placed it against the car door. The door clicked open. 'Luckily, they have a backup system for people like you.' He activated the falcon wing back doors and Katja watched as they swung up over the Tesla. 'That's just showing off.' 'Cool, ya?' Hoog said. 'Boys and their toys,' Katja replied.

Hoog guided Bakker into the back seat and handcuffed him to a steel loop poking out between the rear seats. He handed a small black holdall to Katja. 'Stick that in the front footwell for now.'

Katja hefted the bag. 'Is this your normal boy scout kit?'

'Of course. Jump leads, foot pump, torch, tow rope and pry bar.' Katja shook her head, opened the passenger door and slid the holdall into the footwell before climbing in after it. She shuffled her feet around the bag, making herself comfortable.

'If I'd paid a fortune for a car I think I'd probably want more roadside assistance than a bag of tools,' Katja said.

'You know me. Failing to plan is planning to fail,' Hoog said, as he walked around the car and climbed in behind the wheel.

Katja looked around the interior. 'Are you sure you're allowed to take this?'

Hoog tapped some settings on the large control screen and pressed the brake pedal, causing the car to start with a low hum. 'We were given it to trial by Tesla.'

Katja shook her head. 'They obviously don't know about your record with cars.'

Hoog reversed out of the parking bay and headed towards the exit. 'Just trying to improve my carbon footprint,' he quipped as the steel gates hummed open.

Katja fastened her seatbelt and looked at the display screen. 'Does it have an ejector seat?'

Hoog turned to her. 'Very funny. No, but it does have 795 brake horsepower, a top speed of 155mph and a 0-60 time of 2.4 seconds in *Ludicrous-plus* mode.'

Katja smiled.'Ludicrous-plus mode?' she said.

Hoog tapped the screen. '*Sports mode* should do us for now.'

Katja looked over. 'I'd go with creep mode until you get out of the city,' she said.

They drove through the gates and headed down Kartuizerinnenstraat before reaching the T-junction at Oude Burg. Hoog looked at Bakker. 'Now would be a good time to tell us where we're going.'

Bakker looked around nervously, chewing his lip before speaking. 'Gentpoort.' Hoog swung right into the city one-way system and followed it round into Woolestraat, over the Dijver canal and along Eekhoustraat. He glanced towards a tea room they occasionally frequented. He couldn't help thinking of a strong coffee and a slab of cake.

Katja saw his look. 'You're going to have to wait for

that particular pleasure. Unless this car has a slice of carrot cake stashed away somewhere.'

Hoog smiled. 'If this was my personal vehicle I would have a boot full.' They took a left into Nieuwe Gentweg and a right into Gentpoortstraat. Ahead of them Hoog saw the twin-peaked towers of the port entrance, one of the four remaining medieval city gates. The interior contained a museum and there was a great view from the top floor. He remembered his father taking him there as a child.

They were soon near enough to see the statue of St Adrian in a niche above the roadway. The statue was meant to protect the city during times of plague. 'Turn right,' Bakker said.

Hoog turned onto the R30 and headed alongside the canal towards Katelinjstraat. He could see Minnewater park in the distance. 'It would be a lot easier if you told us where we were headed,' Hoog said.

Bakker shook his head. 'We agreed I would take you there.' Hoog flicked a look at the rearview mirror, trying to read the expression on Bakker's face.

Katja looked in her mirror, 'Shit! We've got company.' A black Range Rover was closing up behind them, flashing its lights and tailgating the cars in front of it. 'Could just be a dickhead. We don't have any bells and whistles, and people aren't expecting police to be using Tesla's just yet.'

Hoog glanced at the mirror. 'Now there's two of them.' Another Range Rover pulled in behind the first. Hoog increased his speed. All sorts of warning icons began to flash on the display.

'Did you override the limiters on this?' Katja said.

'It was delivered that way. The last thing we need is speeding motorists leaving us behind because of some bureaucratic algorithm.'

Katja looked behind. 'How come they knew where we were going?'

Hoog swerved round a truck. 'No one knew where we were going....we didn't know where we were going. The only person who knows our route is him.' Hoog nodded at Bakker. 'They must have followed us from the station in a less obvious vehicle before the Range Rovers took over. 'Is that what's happening here?' Hoog asked, flicking a look to Bakker in the rearview mirror. 'You're taking us on a wild goose chase so your buddies can break you free?' Bakker said nothing. Katja looked at the Range Rovers behind them. Despite Hoog's best efforts they were closing in. Hoog activated the lights and sirens, trying to clear a space ahead of them. But he was blocked by a truck, allowing one of the Range Rovers to pull alongside. The side window slid down and the snub nose of a Sig Sauer MPX 9mm poked out.

There was a sharp crack and the back passenger window crazed but took the bullet. Hoog stamped on the brakes and pulled in behind the Range Rover. He hit the accelerator and rammed the vehicle. The Range Rover spun out of control, and careered into the opposite carriageway, slamming into the metal barrier and flipping over into the woods beside the road. 'One down,' Hoog said, accelerating past the truck, leaving the second Range Rover behind. 'It doesn't look like they want to break you out, does it?' Katja asked. Bakker looked ashen- faced. 'If this car hadn't been fitted with bulletproof glass you'd be dead by now.' Hoog cut across the carriageway, overtaking another truck on the inside and leaving the Range Rover behind blocked by traffic. 'There's too much traffic for us to shake him off.' Hoog watched the rearview mirror as the remaining Range Rover swung into view.'Time to shake things up a bit,' Hoog said.He swung the wheel and the car spun one hundred and eighty degrees and ended up facing the oncoming traffic. Approaching traffic swerved around them.

The Range Rover slewed into the safety lane and slammed to a halt. The Tesla accelerated back along the carriageway against the direction of the approaching traffic. Katja looked at the steering wheel. Hoog was no longer holding it. The autonomous driving mode was in sole control. Effortlessly avoiding the oncoming traffic as they retraced their route back towards Gentpoort.

Behind them the Range Rover raced down the fast

lane away from them, looking for a way to cut across into the opposing carriageway and continue the pursuit.

Bakker was thrashing around on the back seat. 'You're fucking mad!'

Hoog looked at the receding Range Rover. 'Mad but alive, rather than facing the right way and dead,' he flicked a look behind them. 'Shit! They're on the other carriageway.' The Range Rover had pulled clear of the central barrier, cut across the oncoming traffic and was headed back down the other side parallel to them. The Tesla weaved through the oncoming cars accompanied by flashing lights and blaring horns, until it was in sight of the Gentpoort turning. 'They'll be alongside us in minutes, does this car have any more magic up its sleeve?' Katja asked.

Hoog looked across towards the Range Rover, which was gaining fast along the opposite carriageway. 'Maybe.' Hoog tapped the display screen and took back control of the steering wheel. The Range Rover was less than a hundred feet away from them now. Hoog turned the steering wheel, cut left and rocketed towards the bridge leading off the R30 at the Gentpoort exit. He swerved left across the oncoming traffic and Katja saw the bridge was starting to open.

The Range Rover was parallel to them now and braking hard. Hoog accelerated towards the bridge. Smashing through the barrier pole and clawing its way up the gradient before launching into space. 'Whoa!' Katja felt her stomach lurch as they flew through the air and the Tesla thudded back down onto the road. Hoog flicked a look in the rearview mirror as he fought to control the skidding car. 'Shit!' The dark shape of the Range Rover loomed up behind them. Smashing back down onto the road, and ramming them from behind. Hoog fought with the wheel to regain control of the car. He floored the accelerator and pulled away from the Range Rover...racing through the archway towards Bruges. 'Now what?' Katja asked.

Hoog veered left the wrong way down Gentpoort Straat. The traffic was light, with only a few startled motorists for him to avoid. The Range Rover was closing in on them again. 'We have to shake them off, and fast,' Katja said. 'Without killing any pedestrians or cyclists... not necessarily in that order.' They raced through the quiet street, weaving from side to side, blocking the pursuing Range Rover. If it got ahead of them it would all be over, and not in a good way.

'Do you have a plan?' Katja asked. Hoog swung a right into Schaarstraat, passing Astrid Park before swerving left alongside the Coupure canal, an area he knew well.'Sort of,' he replied. 'Thank God for that,' she said, 'I thought we were just driving around aimlessly.' Hoog gave a grim smile as he hurtled over the canal bridge into Predikherenstraat, accelerated left onto

Langesraat and continued over the canal at Hoogstraat before taking a sharp right into Verversdijk, a narrow, cobbled street running alongside the canal. With the Tesla's tyres screaming, and a screen full of traction control warnings bleating for attention, they rocketed down the road.

Ahead of them Katja saw a badly parked delivery van with a narrow gap between it and the canal. The wing mirrors on the Tesla retracted and she winced as Hoog shot towards the gap. 'Time for *Ludicrous Plus* mode," Hoog said, tapping the control screen. Red icons flashed on the screen as the autonomous driving computer diverted all of the power to the driving wheels on the left side of the car.

She felt herself instinctively leaning to the left and saw Hoog and Bakker doing the same. There was a dull crunch as the Tesla's bodywork scraped along the side of the van, its two right hand wheels hung in space for what seemed like an eternity, and then they were past.

Behind them the Range Rover slammed on its brakes, skidding to a halt inches from the van. She saw a man with a thick neck climb out of the vehicle and head towards the van driver's door.

Hoog slowed down as they continued alongside the canal before reaching the junction with Spinolarie and coming to a halt. 'I really didn't think we were going to make it,' Katja said.

Hoog shrugged. 'That's because you don't like being told what to do by a robot.'

Katja smiled, then said, "Shit!' Hoog didn't have to ask what she meant. He could see the Range Rover bearing down on them in the mirror. 'They must have shifted the van.'

Hoog took off with a screech of tyres and veered left, accelerating beside the canal, heading for Jan Van Eck Square. Katja flicked a look into the wing mirror. She heard the distant crack of a gunshot and the rear window took another bullet. Hoog swerved from side to side trying to prevent them from getting a clean shot and Katja hunched down lower in her seat.

A torrent of bullets peppered the boot lid and the back window again ...they meant business. Hoog threw the Tesla sideways into the square, hurtling clockwise round the parked cars and the statue of Jan Van Eyk, who, had he been alive would have no doubt painted the scene with glee. But he wasn't, so he didn't. Though Bruges was quieter after the Christmas holidays there were still a few tourists running for cover.

Hoog aimed the car at the entrance to the Kraanrie and floored the accelerator. The tyres slithered on the slick cobbles and the Tesla's traction control system kicked in, hurling them out of the square into the Kraanrei behind the Poorters Lodge. Hoog slammed on the brakes and the Tesla spun a hundred and eighty degrees before coming to a halt.

Katja looked at Hoog. 'Are you sure this isn't fitted with ejector seats? Because from where I'm sitting we're pretty much fucked if it doesn't.' As if to support her claim, a hail of lead hammered down the side of the Tesla's bodywork.

'I agree, we've got to get out of here. The bodywork is military grade armour, and the windows are made up of five layers of glass and polycarbonate. But it won't stop that,' Hoog said, looking through the side window.

Fritz braced himself against the bonnet of the Range Rover and swung the German Panzerfaust 3 RGW up, levelling it at the stationary Tesla. The Panzerfaust had a range of 600 metres and could penetrate up to 13 inches of armour. Even though the weapon had no recoil Fritz felt happier leaning against something solid. It also made him less of a target if the passengers decided to make a stand. His boss, Grummel, a shaven-headed gym freak spoke out of the side window.

'What are they doing?'

Fritz shrugged. 'Nothing. Just sitting there.'

Grummel nodded. 'Okay, take the shot.' Fritz looked around. Any tourists or locals had long since fled the square and he could hear the sound of a distant siren. Suddenly the Tesla started to move, and within seconds it was racing noiselessly away from them. Fritz squeezed the trigger.

With its computer-controlled aiming sight and range finder, the Panzerfaust couldn't miss. The missile streaked towards the Tesla, punching through the back window before detonating. Within seconds the Tesla was a blazing inferno. Fritz dropped the disposable launch tube and dived back into the Range Rover. It accelerated across the square and into the Spiegelrei. Fritz looked in the wing mirror and saw a lurid orange light flare across the square.

CHAPTER THIRTY-ONE

Hoog and Katja crouched next to the steel ladder beneath the manhole in the canal tunnel beneath the Kraanrei.

Over the centuries as the city grew, many of the canals had been overarched to allow further building, and now Bruges was crisscrossed with canals that meandered beneath the city streets. Further down the tunnel, a manhole cover glowed dull red with heat. Rivulets of burning rubber, and oil from the blazing Tesla above, fell in fiery necklaces through the dark. Hissing as they landed in the canal water below.

Bakker was handcuffed to the ladder, his face reflecting the realization of his position. His accomplices hadn't come to free him, but to kill him. Katja looked around. 'Just like old times,' Hoog grunted. 'But with less people trying to kill us.'

They'd heard the explosion from above as the RGW destroyed the Tesla and the Range Rover drove off.

'I'm not a fan of self-drive cars, but I must admit to feeling sorry for that poor Tesla,' Katja said.

Hoog stood up and flexed his legs. 'You should write a requiem for it. Something like a Bond theme. The AI who loved me, perhaps.'

'Very funny,' Katja said, as she stood up.

'But I mean it.' Hoog said. 'she, or he, did its best. If it hadn't driven away they'd still be looking for us.' Hoog started to climb up the ladder. Katja handed him the black holdall. 'I take it all back about you and your boy scout kit. I would have seriously messed up my nails trying to get that manhole cover open,' Katja said.'Don't lose any sleep over the Tesla; its data was streamed into the cloud. We'll be able to check all of the footage from the onboard cameras when we get back to the station.' He inched the manhole cover open a crack and looked around. A patrol car sat idling fifty metres away, and two officers with guns drawn were checking around the square.

A fire crew were hosing down the remains of the smoking Tesla. Hoog slid the manhole cover to one side and slowly held his warrant card and badge up.

'Hey! Could do with a hand here,' Hoog shouted.

One of the officers swung his gun in Hoog's direction. 'Keep your hands up where I can see them...'

The officer's eyes widened as he recognized Hoog and lowered his gun, 'Sorry Sir...I thought you were...' he trailed off.

'Dead?' Hoog finished his sentence for him.

'Well, we knew you'd taken the Tesla,' the officer said.

Another patrol car arrived and Ward climbed out. He came over to the officer and spotted Hoog.

'Thank God you're okay...' Ward said.

Katja's voice echoed up from below. 'I'm fine as well thanks,' Katja said. Hoog climbed out and lifted Bakker out of the manhole. Katja climbed out and brushed herself off.

'Been spelunking again I see.' Ward said with a smile. 'Not out of choice. It seems Bakker's friends aren't quite as friendly as he thought they were,' Katja said.

Hoog turned to Ward, 'They must have tailed us out of the station.'

An officer came over carrying a disposable launch tube in his gloved hands. 'It's a German Panzerfaust 3, also known as *Tank Fist*. Disposable RGW, Recoilless Grenade Weapon. Not your average street armament.' The officer looked at the smoking wreckage. 'How did you get out of that?'

Hoog smiled. 'Seems that autonomous vehicles have their uses after all.'

The officer looked back at the remains of the Tesla as he spoke, 'I was looking forwards to driving that.'

Hoog handed him the Tesla key-fob. 'Be my guest.'

CHAPTER THIRTY-TWO

Hoog and Katja sat opposite Chief Nils Janssen in his office back at the station. The Chief was reading a report, occasionally shaking his head.'It could have been a bloodbath,' he said, putting the report down.

Hoog nodded. 'We did our best to prevent any civilian collateral, but as you can see the criminals we were under attack from had few worries on that score.' Janssen sighed. Newly in the post after the death of his predecessor, he'd been hoping to bed down in his position without creating too many ripples. But as he looked over at Hoog and Katja he realized that ship had sailed long ago.

Within a few days they'd chased and injured a petty criminal in a passport scam, uncovered some kind of gold laundering operation, been involved in a high-speed chase down the R30, and finished off with a rocket attack in Jan Van Eyck square; not to mention the destruction of an expensive police vehicle only days after its delivery on trial.

The mayor had wasted no time in telling him that high speed car chases and firefights in the center of the city were exactly the kind of thing he didn't want to see happening. When Janssen had been offered the post in Bruges he had discovered that his predecessor, Chief Pieters was facing an internal investigation concerning his collusion with organized crime gangs. The investigation had been dropped after Pieters apparent suicide and all the evidence buried. It would have been catastrophic to the force's image if anything had been made public.

Chief Janssen was well aware of the grey areas surrounding law and order. In some instances, it was necessary to turn a blind eye to criminality when the alternative was far worse. At the end of the day, organized crime could be safer than disorganized crime. A good example of that was the chaos in Iraq. Its devolvement, and the removal of Saddam Hussein, had made it one of the most dangerous and corrupt countries in the world. Chief Pieters involvement with the criminal underworld was moot, his biggest crime was he got caught.

He looked across the desk at Hoog.'Do you have any

idea why you came under attack?' he asked. 'I don't think we were under attack,' Hoog said, 'I think their target was Bakker. We were just collateral.'

Janssen nodded. 'Well, as a silver lining to this disaster I've had the head of Tesla sales on the phone. They're sending us two more Teslas for evaluation. Seems their sales have gone through the roof since people saw you using the autonomous driving facility to make your escape.'

'Well it undoubtedly saved our lives, that's for sure,' Hoog said. 'And for that I'm very grateful,' Janssen said, before going on. 'However, it seems there's an organized crime gang out there that's hell bent on preventing Bakker from leading us to their operation.'Yes, the scale of the attack shows how serious they are,' Katja said. 'We'll interrogate him again. It's more likely he'll want to cooperate now he knows their intentions,' Hoog said.

Janssen shuffled through some front-page proofs of the next day's newspapers from a pile on his desk.

'The editors have been kind enough to show me what's coming up in tomorrow's papers.

This is my favourite.' He held up the front page of a local newspaper.

"Detectives Escape Carmageddon!"

'The way things are going I wouldn't be surprised if James Bond ends up driving a Tesla in his next movie,' Katja said.

Hoog looked at her and shook his head. 'That's not going to happen. It would be like having him ask for a diet coke rather than a Martini.'

'Or there being a female Dr. Who,' Katja said with a smile.

Janssen put the paper down. 'If I can interrupt your debate on pop culture for a moment...what's your next move?'

Hoog shrugged. 'We may get some leads from the Tesla camera footage, the CCTV from the Square and anything that goes online from the general public. Though to be fair there weren't that many people around.'

Janssen nodded. 'Okay, let me know if you find out anything more from Bakker and I'll flag up a request for a safe house with the protection unit in case he wants to deal.'

Hoog stood up. 'Thanks Chief.' Janssen watched as Hoog and Katja left his office and headed towards the interview room beneath the station.

Katja turned to Hoog as they walked down the stone steps leading to the catacombs. Originally part of a Carthusian Convent dating back to the 15th century, the catacombs now provided ad hoc offices, an interview room and a firing range. 'Do you think we'll get anything out of him this time?' she said. 'I'm not leaving the room until we do,' Hoog replied.

CHAPTER THIRTY-THREE

Bakker sat slumped in the police station interview room, picking at a piece of loose skin on one of his fingers. He was trying to play the hard man, but his near-death experience had clearly shaken him. Bakker's lawyer sat hunched in the seat next to him. The intervening time had done nothing to improve the lack of enthusiasm for his client. Hoog tapped the record button on the machine. 'For the record, this is Detective Jochum Hoog and Katja Blondell interviewing Nils Bakker.' The recorder beeped. Hoog flicked through a sheaf of printouts before speaking. 'Now that we're clear what's at stake, don't you think you should tell us where the operation is being run from?'

Bakker shook his head. 'I don't know where it is.

When I was taken there I was blindfolded, and the mask was only taken off once I was inside the foundry.'

'How long was your journey?' Hoog asked. He knew that if they had a rough timing they could establish a perimeter to narrow down the possible locations of the foundry. 'About an hour's drive,' Bakker said. 'Why were you at the foundry?' Katja asked. Bakker rubbed his face. His shoulders slumped as he remembered back. 'They came to my shop a few months ago. They said they had a business proposition for me. From the way they talked it was obvious they weren't going to accept no for an answer.''They wanted you to dive on the sub,' Hoog said.

'Yes.' 'How did they know there was gold in the sub? Katja asked.'I didn't ask. These aren't the sort of people you chat with. You do what they say and don't ask any questions. I got the impression they did that sort of thing for a living.''Like treasure hunters?' Hoog said.'Yes, but more official, like they had a big organization behind them. They definitely weren't amateurs. That's why I didn't ask them anything. What you don't know can't hurt you,' Bakker said.'Unless of course you're looking down the barrel of a rocket guided weapon,' Hoog said.

'They must have thought I'd ratted them out,' Bakker said.'I don't see how. After all, you didn't know where they were operating from, only that it was a foundry,' Hoog said.

Bakker shrugged. 'As I said, there's no reasoning with people like that,' he paused. 'All I knew was they wanted me to cut a hole in the side of the sub to allow access for the dredger.''Presumably they offered to pay you for your services, and your silence?' Hoog said.'Yes,' Bakker mumbled.'So...the foundry. When did you go there?' Bakker looked scared. As if the question had stirred up something he'd rather not revisit. He took a deep breath before speaking. 'It was a few days after the dive.''During which you liberated a few of the ingots for your own personal use?' Hoog said.'Yes. I reckoned if I was smart, I could make enough from the gold to leave the country and start a new life.''But they were smarter, and you realized you were going to have to leave the country faster than you'd planned, which is when you started collecting passports,' Hoog said, holding up a couple of water damaged passports.

'Yes. It wasn't the best idea I've ever had.''For sure. Go on,' Hoog said.'They drove me to the foundry and once I was inside they took the mask off.''What did you see?' Hoog asked.

Bakker flashed back to the night they'd come for him. He'd been cataloguing some Egyptian artefacts at the back of his shop when the bell rang. It was too late for a normal customer, but sometimes a friend would turn up and they'd go out for a drink. He went to the front entrance and looked through the spyhole. He'd barely had time to register a thickset man when the door was kicked open.

Three men had stormed in and pinned him down. They tied his hands together, jammed a mask over his head and dragged him outside. He was bundled onto a cold metal floor in the back of a van and driven off.

An hour later, freezing, and bruised from the twisting and turning route to get out of the city, the van had come to a halt. He was dragged out and manhandled through a doorway into a large open space, filled with the echoing sound of heavy machinery, acrid fumes and heat. His mask was ripped off, and he found himself standing in a vast industrial shed.

He glimpsed various statues and pieces of scrap metal in the shadows surrounding a large blast furnace, the source of the heat.

About fifteen men were working at the foundry, and in their silver suits and reflective heatproof helmets they looked like performers in some grotesque slow-motion theatre play set in the future. Bakker looked at Hoog and continued.

'Everyone was wearing full protective gear and reflective visors with helmets. They could have been Martians for all I knew,' Bakker said.'So why were you there?' Hoog said.'They led me over to the furnace. I saw two men drag another man towards it. A large man with a heavy Russian accent came over to me. He waved a gold ingot at me. He told me that the man had stolen it from the foundry...'

Bakker stopped talking. He swallowed. His eyes filled with terror at the memory. 'They threw him into the fucking furnace. I'll never forget the sound he made...or the smell.'

'They were sending you a message,' Hoog said, 'showing you what would happen if you stole from them or betrayed them...'

Bakker looked at him. 'Now do you understand why I lied to you? They don't care if I've told you anything, they're going to kill me anyway.'

Katja put a hand on his shoulder.'We'll protect you. But we still need to find them.' Hoog reached across and switched off the recorder.

'Is that it?' Bakker asked. 'I thought we had a deal?''We do. The thing is your last deal nearly got us all killed, so you can see why we might have a few trust issues.''They tried to kill me as well,' Bakker said.'Yes, but that's not exactly mitigating circumstances. It's like a suicide bomber complaining he's nearer to the blast than you.''So, what happens next?' Bakker said.'You'll be held in custody overnight while we organize a safe house. If we locate their base of operations we may need to conduct a further interview with you for identification purposes.'

Bakker stared at Hoog. 'You can't put me in the same room as those monsters,' he said.

Hoog shook his head. 'Obviously not, we'll be using a video link. If you still had your mobile phone we could have tracked your movements and located the foundry that way.''They threw it into the furnace along with that poor bastard,' Bakker said. 'Better the phone than you, eh?' Hoog said grimly. He gathered up his files and went to the door. He tapped on it and two officers came in and escorted Bakker out.

I almost felt sorry for him,' Katja said as they climbed the stone steps leading back up into the reception area. 'You'll get over it,' Hoog said. 'A rocket launcher has a polarizing effect on one's viewpoint.' They walked past the reception desk. 'Night Sophia,' Katja said.

Sophia looked up. 'You too. And don't do anything I wouldn't,' she said with a smile. 'That gives us a lot of scope,' Katja said, as they opened the glass doors and stepped out into the street.

Sophia had been her confidant during her breakup with Hoog, and had helped her through many a dark night before her transfer to Antwerp and the recent renewal of their relationship.'I could murder a waffle,' Hoog cut into her thoughts.

‘That’s just what the public wants to hear. A detective planning his next murder,’ Katja said. ‘Do you think we’ll be able to track down where the foundry is?’ she continued.‘I’m sure Ward will come up with something. According to him everything leaves a digital footprint, it’s just a matter of tracking it down.’

‘Won’t they have packed up and gone by tomorrow? Katja asked.‘I don’t think so. They must know Bakker can’t tell us where they’re based, and given the size of the operation it’ll take some time to pull out without attracting attention. If they’re still working when we find them we can put them under observation, track them and shut down the whole operation.’‘Bridge of Sighs here I come,’ Katja said.‘I’ll drink to that,’ Hoog said.

They headed towards the market and the sound of a distant accordion. A man was sitting next to a wheeled cart in Woolestraat playing a medley of popular tunes. A small black dog with a white patch of fur over one eye lay with his head resting on the man’s feet.

Katja dropped some change into a battered felt hat on the ground in front of him. He nodded his thanks. Katja stood looking at Hoog.

He fumbled in his pockets for some change, eventually pulling out a crumpled five euro note. He looked at it and hesitated. 'You want change?' Katja said, giving him a pitying smile. Hoog dropped the note into the man's hat and stroked the dog before moving on.'I do have waffles in my flat, as well as other treats,' Katja said.

Hoog leaned down and gave her a kiss. The accordion player segued into a lilting rendition of James Blunt's 'You're Beautiful.''Everyone's a smartarse,' Hoog said, breaking off from his kiss. 'I'll take that as a yes,' Katja said

They headed down Woolestraat past the chocolate shops and the children's toy shop, a strange bedfellow situated next to the sex shop, and soon reached the entrance to the Torture Museum and its wooden stocks. Katja had been lent the flat above the museum by an old friend when she'd transferred from Antwerp, and liked its quirky location. She tapped the key pad and the door clicked open.

They climbed the stone steps up to the second floor and Katja tapped another keypad before heading into the flat. 'Coffee, alcohol, or...?''I'll take the third option,' Hoog said, moving over to her and stroking her neck before leaning in for another kiss.

Katja smiled. 'Don't you think it's about time you thought about living on dry land?' she said with a smile.

Hoog looked at her. 'Would there be some sub-text to that question?''Well spotted. Yes, I would like to be sharing somewhere with you that didn't move around like a giant creaking waterbed.''We've had a lot of fun on that old creaking waterbed,' Hoog said.'I'm not denying it. But a lot of water has gone under a lot of bridges since then, and I think it might be a good time to move things onto a more stable foundation.''Are you asking me to move in with you?' Hoog said.'You're the detective, you can work that out,' Katja said with a smile. Hoog thought about this. She was right of course, and her recent near-death experience had confirmed how much Katja meant to him.

'I will have a drink, and you're right. We could get somewhere together and I could rent out the barge through Airbnb or something similar.'

Katja went into the fridge and pulled out a bottle of white wine. She uncorked it and filled two glasses, handing Hoog one and raising the other one.'To dry land.' Hoog tapped her glass.

They finished their glasses, and Hoog re-filled them.'I'm glad you're moving on. I was getting worried you'd end up mirroring more and more popular TV detectives until I barely recognized you,' Katja said.

'What do you mean?' Hoog asked, finishing his

glass.'Well there's the Van Der Valk houseboat you live on, then there's your drumming hobby mirroring Liese Meerhout, the drumming detective in *Rough Justice*...what next? Are you going to start leaning round the door in a raincoat and asking the *Columbo* case solving question?' 'You're too young to know anything about *Columbo*,' Hoog said, smiling.'That's for sure, but my dad was a huge fan of his, along with *Diagnosis Murder* and *Monk*,' Katja went over and gave Hoog a hug.'Sorry, that's unkind. I just think you need to big up the uniqueness of the Hoog brand,' she said.'I already have the highest case clear up rate in West Flanders, I suppose I could listen to classical music...''Very funny, my dad used to watch Morse as well.'

Katja put her glass down and walked through the door into the bedroom, closing it behind her. Hoog looked at the door, trying to work out his next move. The door half opened and Katja peered out from behind it and spoke in a pastiche of Colombo's American accent. 'Just one more thing. Who do I have to kill around here to get some attention?'

CHAPTER THIRTY-FOUR

Sophia was finishing her final cup of coffee for the evening and preparing to leave the station when the phone rang. She cursed the timing, put her mug down and picked up the phone. It was Kurt. He was excitable and mysterious in equal measure, and after five minutes it was obvious he wasn't going to be fobbed off. He claimed to have a lead on the missing 't Zand square statues, and was convinced that with immediate action they could solve the case. Against her better judgement she'd agreed to meet him.

Fifteen minutes later Sophia was parking alongside the Gentpoort fort entrance and walking over to the small door to one side. She pressed the *Caretaker* button on the intercom beside the door and waited. The speaker crackled and a tinny voice spilled out.

'Sophia?'

'Unless you're expecting someone else,' Sophia said. She was already regretting her decision. It was cold, and she was tired. The door buzzed and she pushed it open. A set of narrow stone stairs led up to the Museum level. Kurt appeared at the other side of a display of heraldry in a glass case. 'Thank you for coming. My office is this way.'

Sophia followed Kurt through an ancient oak door festooned with wrought iron bolts and up another set of stone steps into a small room, with arrow slits through which she could see the lights of Bruges winking in the distance.

The description of his workplace as an office was wildly optimistic. It was about the size of a toilet with a desk squashed against one wall. There was a one ring cooker, a fan heater and a kettle. And a bunk bed was folded up in one corner. But none of this was of any interest to her.

What did interest her was a large corkboard covering one wall. On it were pictures and Google Earth print-outs of various foundries around Bruges. Below them were a series of photographs of various statues including those stolen from 't Zand square sculpted by Stefaan Depuydt and Livia Canestraro.

'Coffee?' Kurt asked. 'Thanks, milk and two.' Sophia looked around the room. Despite the confines of his office Kurt kept the space immaculate. She wondered if he had compulsive obsessive behavior along with his conspiracy and prepper personality.

As Hoog had said, his disheveled appearance was not accompanied by poor personal hygiene, but was part of the contrived image he cultivated to enable him to blend into the background. She waved a hand at the cork-board. 'Is this your latest conspiracy?' 'Yes.''So, what is it?' Sophia asked. Kurt fixed her with his pale blue eyes.

'Well, for the past few years I've been monitoring the global thefts of large bronze statues. Mother and Child from Berlin; Four Horsemen of the Apocalypse, Paris; The Angel, Budapest; Birds of Prey, Singapore; Christ Sleeping, London...and of course the 't Zand Square theft.' Sophia looked at the other pictures, as Kurt went on.

'I could see a pattern emerging. At first I thought it might have been an insurance scam...or maybe they were being stolen to order for some millionaire with a huge estate.'

'So what was the pattern?' Sophia said.'The pattern was, that after a few months the stolen statues would reappear. The police would get a tip-off leading to their whereabouts and the statue would be returned to its original site,' Kurt said.'So it was an insurance scam?''No. I checked the insurance companies and the original payouts were always handed back once the statue was recovered.' 'So, you never got to the bottom of the conspiracy?'

Kurt slid his fingers across the laptop tracker pad. 'No. But after the theft from t' Zand square I did some research on other countries where foundries were initially idle at the time of the previous thefts.''What do you mean idle?' Sophia said. 'Well, when foundries are shut down they try to keep the furnace ticking over in case they can be saved. Starting a foundry up that has been completely shut down costs millions, so even after companies have gone into administration they only switch off the furnace as a last resort.'

Sophia nodded. 'They're hoping someone will take them over or the government will bail them out?'

'Yes. I did some chronological thermal analysis on idling foundries nearest to the site of the thefts.'

Kurt tapped a key on his laptop and the screen filled with satellite imagery displaying colour readouts of each countries infrared spectrum.

'What am I looking at?' Sophia asked.'Landsat infrared satellite pictures. They show the thermal output from idling foundries in the various countries during the months before and after the theft of statues.'

Sophia looked at the screen as Kurt flicked between the time scales and the countries involved.'So, their thermal footprint spikes for a month after the theft, then drops back down when the stolen statue reappears.'

Sophia said.'Yes. The thermal footprint also matches up with power surges.''How did you track those?''I have a friend who works at the power station in Noordekempen; he gave me details of power spikes that matched up with the thermal surges from the same foundries,' Kurt said.'So, you thought they were melting down the stolen statues?' Sophia said.'That was one theory. But when the statues started to reappear it became obvious that wasn't what was going on.''So what do you think is going on?' Sophia asked.'That's what I've been trying to find out. But, even though I could monitor other countries virtually, I couldn't actually be there to investigate in person.' 'Until the t' Zand square statues were stolen,' Sophia said.'Yes. I was expecting to see the same pattern here and be able to investigate the source of the spike for myself in real time.''But it didn't happen,' Sophia said. 'No. Nothing happened for over a year.''Until today.' Sophia said.'Yes, earlier tonight one of the foundries I was monitoring near Maldegem had a power surge followed by a thermal spike.'You think someone's using the foundry illegally?'

'I think we should check it out,'. Kurt said.'We?' Sophia said.

Kurt smiled. 'I thought initially we could recce the place and if something's going on you could call for backup. That way, if this is just one of my misguided conspiracy theories you won't look foolish to your boss.'You think we can catch them in the act? Whatever their act is,' Sophia said.'Exactly. You get to make an arrest and shut down a global operation and I get to solve a conspiracy.'

Kurt went over to his makeshift corkboard and tapped a list. 'Conspiracy theories are rarely solved, and when they are, it can take centuries to unravel the cover-up. We've only really just found out what happened leading up to the Titanic's sinking back in 1912.'One of Hoog's favourite subjects, though I think he described it as Carl Jung's theory of synchronicity, or was that Einstein's quantum entanglement, or spooky action at a distance, as he called it?' Sophia said. 'Yes, he's a bit of a fan of that one. Quantum entanglement is when you're about to phone your mother or your partner and just before you punch in the number they call you.'That's for sure. Though that wouldn't be hard given how many times my mother rings me.'I can imagine,' Kurt said, continuing. 'There are many conspiracies that will never be solved. The assassination of JFK, the Twin Towers attack, Port Chicago, the death of Princess Diana...I could go on.'

'Please don't,' Sophia said. 'But I haven't heard about Port Chicago.'

Kurt nodded. 'It was a huge explosion that took place in a ship being loaded with munitions in July 1940. Conspiracists believe it was an atomic bomb because of the mushroom cloud it produced. Hard core conspiracists say it was an atomic bomb in one of the ships detonated to measure its effects. The men were used as guinea pigs. Two hundred and twenty of the men killed were African Americans.'

'That's one hell of a conspiracy,' Sophia said. 'How do you sleep at night? Knowing all this stuff. It gives me the creeps just thinking about it.''I live alone,' Kurt said. A sad smile flitted across his face, and then was gone. 'But using people as guinea pigs...could they really have got away with that?' Sophia asked. 'A good conspiracy is unprovable,' Kurt said.'Which is why you're so keen to catch these criminals in the act. You think you'll be stopping a conspiracy before it becomes an unprovable one,' Sophia said.'Exactly. And, it would make a great chapter in my conspiracy book.' 'What's it called?''*Trust no one*,' Kurt said.'Good title. I look forward to seeing Mulder and Scully on the red carpet at the film premier.''I wish,' Kurt said. Sophia looked at her watch. It was eleven o'clock. She could walk away now, get Kurt to file a report in the morning, and be safely tucked up in bed by midnight.

She remembered Hoog's remarks back at the station, when he'd suggested Kurt could help her solve some cases, and how it might help her chances at making Detective Inspector. Throughout her career one thing had always trumped evidence and that was her gut feeling. Also, despite the fact that Kurt was without a doubt a serious conspiracy nut, Hoog had a point, it wouldn't do her career any harm to shut down a large-scale criminal enterprise. Recovering the 't Zand Square statues couldn't harm her profile in the local press either.'Okay. We'll check out the foundry site. But if there's something going on, I'll call for backup.'

Kurt nodded, 'of course,' he said.

And in that split second, she made one of the worst decisions of her life.

CHAPTER THIRTY-FIVE

Kurt and Sophia headed down the cramped stone stairs curling around the ancient towers, back through the museum, and out into the chilly night. Tendrils of fog hung in the air over the canal and the full moon silvered the surface of the water. Kurt locked the door behind him and they walked across the road to his car, a beaten-up classic Volvo 245 station wagon in a rusty beige. As they climbed in, the smell of old leather stirred Sophia's memories of riding in her dad's old Volvo as a young girl. Kurt churned the starter motor, sending a gout of smoke belching out of the exhaust. They headed across the bridge and onto the R30 ring road as Sophia settled in for the ride.

Half an hour later they were heading down the R9 towards the town of Maldegem. By then Kurt had exhausted his conspiracy theories and she'd learned more about him as a person.

During the height of the 2008 banking crisis, as the homeless epidemic reached a crisis point in the city Kurt had taken action. As a long time prepper he'd stashed away piles of tinned food, pasta, rice and bottled water. He was ready for World War Three, but that event had been trumped by the worldwide financial crisis.

Kurt had spent his evenings handing out supplies to the homeless until he'd fallen foul of an overzealous officer that had ticketed him for illegal parking. After a brief tussle he'd been arrested and spent the night in jail. This was before Sophia had been transferred from Ghent to Bruges, so she'd been unaware of his exploits.

The more she learned about Kurt the more she liked him. He was certainly a million miles away from the disheveled nut job most people took him for.'Did they charge you with anything?' Sophia asked.

Kurt looked across at her, 'They were going to, but then Hoog turned up. He managed to convince the arresting officer that it wouldn't be good for the department's image if the press found out they'd jailed someone trying to help the homeless.'

Sophia nodded. This knowledge explained Hoog's bond with Kurt. 'Good for you. What happened after they released you?' Sophia asked. 'They set up a food bank and gave me special dispensation to organize a regular food run for the homeless at night to alleviate the situation.' Kurt flicked the indicator down and they turned off the R9 and headed towards Maldegem town centre.

Though its history stretched back to the 16th century Maldegem was not as busy as the tourist hotspot of Bruges. Its biggest attraction was the Steam Train museum, though it had a pleasant enough market square with a fountain and a statue of Salomon Van Maldeghem, an armoured crusader on a prancing horse.

It was past midnight as they drove through the deserted town. They wound their way through the quiet streets and were soon leaving the town, passing the Sint-Anna-park and heading towards the industrial area on the outskirts of the town.

'What's the name of this place?' Sophia asked.

Kurt looked down at a piece of paper on his lap. 'Zwaan Steel. It's not far.'

Sophia closed her eyes. Sitting in the warm leather womb of the Volvo she was finding it hard to stay awake.

She must have dozed off because when she opened her eyes and looked over at Kurt, he was still knee deep in the world of conspiracies. The one she'd woken to was a future where a combination of pollution and global warming had caused the ice caps to melt, releasing a primordial virus into the planet's atmosphere where it used the jet stream to spread across the world wiping out the human race. She pretended to have been listening

'Well, let's hope that doesn't happen anytime soon. Besides, I doubt any virus would survive a journey in the jet stream,' Sophia said. Kurt smiled. 'It's only a theory, though I have no doubt there are all sorts of nasty bugs that have been lurking under the ice for millions of years,' he paused. 'Have you heard of the Fu-Go balloon bombs?'

Sophia shook her head and secretly prayed they were near their destination. 'No, I haven't. But I'm guessing you have?'

Kurt grinned. 'Of course. During the second world war the Imperial Japanese Navy developed a hydrogen balloon to drop bombs on America. They intended using the jet stream over the Pacific Ocean to drop them on North American cities.'

Sophia nodded. 'That's impressive.'

'Yes. The Japanese fire balloon carried out the longest range attacks ever conducted in the history of warfare. A record that remained unbroken until the 1982 Falklands War raids. They launched about ten thousand of them.'

'How come I never heard of them?' Sophia said.

'They weren't very successful because of the unpredictability of the weather. Only about three hundred of them were seen, and there were only six people killed when they decided to touch the balloons and they blew up.'

Sophia looked over at Kurt. He was like a giant sponge absorbing all of the global conspiracies floating around on the internet, in chat rooms and social media. She was sure his virus theory was from some TV show he'd watched and forgotten about, only to recycle it into one of his conspiracies further down the line. The Volvo slowed and Kurt pointed through the windscreen, 'There it is.'

In the distance she saw a large metal shed.

"ZWAAN STEEL FOUNDRY AND CASTINGS"

was displayed in flaking white paint on the front of the building. There was an unmanned security hut and a single pole barrier. A few street lights smeared the foundry car park with a dirty yellow tint.

'We should park further down the street,' Sophia said. Kurt drove past the foundry and swung the Volvo into a small car park, killed the engine and switched off the lights. They sat there as the hot engine ticked beneath the bonnet.

'What now?' Kurt asked.

'Let's just lie low for a bit. There might be a security routine around the perimeter,' Sophia said. They sat there in the cooling interior of the Volvo, watching the area around the foundry. Kurt reached into a glove compartment and pulled out a bag of Maltesers. 'Sweet?' Sophia smiled. 'You think of everything.'

'I'm a prepper, what do you expect?' Kurt said with a grin.

Sophia tilted the bag and emptied a couple of Maltesers into her hand. 'I don't suppose you have a set of infra-red goggles lying around?'

Kurt reached under his seat and pulled out a small bag. He slid out a couple of pairs of hi-tech devices resembling binoculars with electronic controls. He handed a pair to Sophia. 'Ultra-night vision infrared recording goggles.'

Sophia studied the controls and tapped a button. A red glow leaked from the eyepieces of the device. 'You really do come prepared.' Sophia scanned the security hut and the car park. She saw a small red shape under one of the parked cars. 'I have a contact at twelve-o' clock...'

Kurt fired his goggles up and looked. 'Either a very large rat...or a cat.'

Sophia tilted her head up at the building. She saw a plume of heat spiralling into the night sky.

Kurt was right. The foundry was much hotter than it would be if the furnace was just ticking over.

'Okay. I think we should move nearer. We'll spot anybody with the goggles before they see us.'

They climbed out of the car and crept towards the back of the building, which lay in shadow. There was a small metal door set into the main entrance gate. Sophia produced a wallet holding a selection of lock picks from her pocket.

'Cool,' Kurt said.

'Sometimes it's quicker than a warrant,' Sophia said. She inserted a small tension wrench into the tumbler lock.

'Just need to scrub the pins with my rake.' She jiggled the rake and there was a soft click from the lock. She carefully eased the door open. She froze as the door gave out a muffled shriek. But the roar of the furnace masked any sound and they slipped inside. Apart from the dull glow of the furnace the plant was shrouded in darkness. Sophia looked around. There was a symbol and a sign pointing to a washroom at the end of a row of oxygen tanks. 'We need to be another tree in the forest,' she said. They headed towards the door and opened it.

The room was a narrow cubicle lined with some metal lockers and pegs, showers and toilet facilities. Hanging up at one end were some silvered heat resistant suits with protective helmets and bronze tinted glass.

They went over to the suits and after some trial and error managed to find two that fitted. Sophia pulled out her Glock 19 and two sets of cuffs and slipped them into one of the pouch pockets in the suit. Kurt looked at the Glock. 'Do you think you'll need that?'

'Not unless somebody comes at me,' Sophia said picking, up her helmet. 'Stay behind me,' Sophia said, heading out of the washroom and along a small corridor towards a door with an inset glass porthole leading into the main foundry. She held up a hand for Kurt to stop, and peered through the grimy glass.

She saw a vast bucket-shaped foundry ladle filled with white hot, molten, glowing metal moving ponderously through the air. The ladle hung from steel wires connected to a massive gantry crane running the width of the foundry, trailing smoke and sparks as it rumbled through the air.

A man in full protective gear walked to one side beneath it with a remote in his hand controlling its progress. She could make out six or seven men spread around the floor.

One man drove a forklift truck loaded with a metal container slowly towards the furnace. The contents glowed a dull yellow in the reflected light from the furnace.

'What does that look like to you?' Kurt leaned over to peer through the porthole. Bathed in the blood red light of the furnace and showered by the waterfall of sparks from the ladle, the scene resembled a satanic witch's kitchen. 'It could be gold,' he said.

Sophia strained to see in the gloom. 'I can't see from this angle.'

'These do have a zoom lens you know,' Kurt said, holding up the infrared googles. Sophia gave him a look and took the goggles. She scanned the floor trying to get a clean view of the container contents on the forklift.'I need to be higher or closer. Stay behind me,' Sophia said. She checked that the men in protective gear were focused on the transfer ladle, slipped through the door and headed round some loose pallets stacked with wheel castings. They ducked behind the wall and headed between the piles of moulds. 'Get ready to put your helmet on,' Sophia said. She looked down at the front of her suit and saw a name embossed on the material. *Gert Frome.* Kurt's bore the name *Nils Groller*. She imagined these were the names of the original workers employed before the plant went into administration.

She turned to Kurt.'If we get stopped and anyone speaks to us you'd better answer. I doubt there's ever been any women working here.'

Kurt nodded. 'They'd have more sense than to work in this hell hole. I don't think I'll be able to make any kind of believable conversation if one of them spots us.'

'No, I imagine not. They must be able to identify each other somehow.' Sophia tapped her pocket. 'Don't worry. If it gets awkward they can always speak to Heer Glock.' 'Maybe they've stuck different names on their suits or they wear armbands while they're working here.'

'In which case we're fucked,' Sophia said. They reached the end of the wall of stacked moulds. Sophia peered round a large mould and looked out across the floor of the foundry. The transfer ladle had halted over a sand mould on the floor beneath it. The man with the remote was guiding it lower, positioning the ladle above the hole in the mould.

From where she stood Sophia couldn't make out whether the mould was a complete entity or part of something larger. She leaned back into the shadows as the forklift truck rumbled past with its load.

She saw its cargo. Gold ingots. And in that second Kurt's stolen statue conspiracy took a massive leap into Hoogs ongoing investigation. She ducked back behind the moulds.'What is it?' Kurt asked. He could see from her face that she'd seen something. 'They're definitely using gold ingots for something,'

Kurt nodded. 'They could be melting it down to make it easier to transport out of the country. As long as they treat whatever it is to make it look like bronze or some other metal, no one's going to give them a second look.'

'And when they get to where they're going, recast it into ingots,' Sophia said.

'That makes sense, but it's not the sort of conspiracy I was expecting,' Kurt said.'I wouldn't worry about that. I'll make sure you get the recognition you deserve on this case. They might even make you a statue. Hoog will be more than happy to get his case closed. He's been desperate to get out to Venice and join his colleague's investigation.' Kurt's ears pricked up.

'What case is that?' he asked.

Sophia smiled, 'If I told you that I'd have to kill you.'

'If it was a good conspiracy I'd die happy.'

Sophia's expression suddenly changed. 'Put your helmet on.' Kurt jammed his helmet on and Sophia followed suit. One of the men was looking in their direction. 'He may have seen us,' Sophia said. 'Grab a casting.' They bent down and picked up some kind of drive shaft before standing up. The man walked over and halted in front of them. 'What the fuck are you doing with that?' Kurt flashed a look to Sophia. He realized it was a pointless action as their tinted visors made it impossible to see any expression. 'We were told to clean up the area,' Kurt said. It was the vaguest reply he could think of. The man cocked his visor at them. Sophia could imagine his eyes narrowing as he looked at the names on their suits. 'Who told you to clean up the area. Who are you?' the man asked, his tone angry. 'Who are you?' Kurt fired back.

He knew this tactic had a limited lifespan. He felt Sophia pulling at the casting they held and followed her lead. He released his hold on the casting and stepped back as Sophia slammed the heavy object into the man's helmet before following it up with a sweeping leg that smashed into his knees, sending him tumbling to the floor, howling in agony. She stamped her foot into the small of his back, scooped a pair of handcuffs from her pocket and chucked them to Kurt.

'Cuff him.'

The man groaned, his shattered visor shedding pieces of acrylic as they hauled him into an upright position. They manhandled him behind the wall of castings and refastened his hands through a heavy casting. Sophia pulled the remains of his helmet and visor from his head.

The man's eyes blazed with anger, 'You're dead,' he spat out.

'Not yet,' Sophia said. She pulled the Glock from her pocket and pressed the barrel against his forehead hard enough to leave an angry red mark. She produced her warrant card and held it in front of his face. 'What are you doing here?' The man said nothing.

'Hard man eh?' Sophia said. 'You'll soon know,' the man said, giving a smile composed of badly tended teeth.

Sophia shook her head. 'I'd advise you to drop the threats and start talking,' she said, cocking the Glock.

'No comment,' the man said.'You're way too early to play the legal representative card my friend. You're more at the stage of being shot accidentally in self-defence because you were in the wrong place at the wrong time. What we call collateral. Your friends won't even hear the shot.'

The anger went out of the man's eyes and was replaced with doubt. 'You can't shoot me, you're a police officer.'

Sophia gave him her best mad look. 'Yes, but my friend here isn't. I could give him my gun to keep you under control and he might get nervous and accidentally shoot you.'

Kurt took his helmet off and looked at the man. 'She's right. I do get nervous.'

The man sat on the foundry floor glaring at them with bloodshot eyes. He wasn't giving anything away. Whatever he was hiding it was obvious that his fear of revealing it was far greater than a Glock-induced fatality. 'Okay, we get the picture. Looks like we'll have to leave you here and find out what's going on for ourselves. Sophia took her helmet and jammed it onto the man's head. 'Don't go anywhere,' she turned to Kurt, 'I suggest we dump our gear and travel light. If we get into a fight I want to be able to move faster than them,'

Kurt nodded. 'I agree.' They shed their protective clothing and retraced their steps back towards the changing room. Sophia looked at her watch. It was one o' clock in the morning and she could feel her energy levels dropping.

'What now?' Kurt whispered, then repeated himself when he remembered the satanic sound levels in the foundry. Sophia looked out over the foundry floor. Four or five men were standing round the mouth of the furnace wearing protective gear. One of them opened the door and thrust a long metal shaft with a small scraper on the end into the mouth of the furnace. He scraped out red hot slag into a collection trough below the lip of the furnace, sending sparks swirling around the opening.

A giant of a man with a shaven-head and a familiar face walked towards something under a tarpaulin near the main entrance to the foundry. Sophia leaned nearer to Kurt. 'What do you think is under that tarpaulin?'

Kurt didn't hesitate. 'My best guess is it's a statue waiting to be melted down.'

'So you think there are two things going on here.

Statues being melted down for scrap and some kind of gold laundering operation,' Sophia said.

Kurt shrugged. 'It looks that way, but it doesn't make a lot of sense. I can understand the gold being melted down as they need to conceal its origins. But I don't know why they would be melting the statue down…'

'Perhaps they're just storing it,' Sophia said. 'It's possible, but that doesn't fit my theory. Up until now all of the stolen statues have been returned. But the 't Zand statues have been missing since 2018; why keep them for so long.' Sophia flicked a look towards the tarpaulin. 'As you said, most conspiracy theories are never solved.'

Sophia looked around the floor of the foundry. The giant had disappeared. Where was he? Her question was soon answered.

'Hey!'

He was standing above them on the gantry that ran around the wall, high above the foundry. His voice was audible even above the roar of the furnace. Sophia dismissed him from her internal threat list. It would take him time to climb back down, and even if he was armed the chances of him hitting them was low.

The men by the floor mould controlling the pour from the gantry conversion ladle looked up from their task, trying to place the origin of the shout. One of them turned and looked up at the giant on the gantry. The giant pointed in Sophia's direction. 'Move,' she said to Kurt. They ducked behind the wall of stacked moulds and kept moving until she was sure they were out of the giant's sight. 'What now?' Kurt asked. He'd seen the men and knew their escape plan was compromised; not that they'd had an escape plan, but at least they'd had the advantage of surprise. 'Circle back to where we came in and get the hell out of here,' Sophia said. It had seemed like a good plan until they reached the washroom door and found it locked with a keypad blocking their access.

'What are you doing?' A muffled voice came from behind them. Sophia looked towards the mask of the person standing in protective gear behind them. She closed the gap between them in two strides. 'Can't hear you,' she cocked her ear theatrically. The man began to say something but gave up when Sophia slammed her foot into the side of his knee, sending him crashing to the ground. She ripped off his helmet and saw a bearded man with a gap-toothed smile. He wasn't smiling for long. 'What's the combination to the changing room?' Sophia said, pointing her Glock at him.

'Who the fuck are you?' the man managed to get out, before Sophia slammed his head on the floor with a sickening thud. 'Don't make me repeat myself.' '1,2,3,4,' the man said, groaning. 'Good, right up there with your IQ.' Sophia cuffed him to the metal railing that ran around the wall leading to some steps up to the gantry. She flicked a look up into the roof space. The giant had vanished and she was out of cuffs. 'C'mon,' she said. Kurt followed as they swung left back past the changing room entrance. 'Aren't we going out that way?' Kurt asked. 'Keeping it in reserve,' Sophia said. They picked their way past rows of gas cylinders and an untidy pile of welding equipment and protective face masks. 'Isn't it time to call for backup?' Kurt said.

Sophia nodded. 'As soon as we're out,' she said. From their vantage point they had a good view of the foundry floor without being exposed.

'Down there!' The voice of the giant echoed round the foundry. 'Shit,' Sophia said.

The giant had moved down a level and was now the one-eyed giant in a very noisy kingdom of the blind. He was acting as a spotter for his men on the ground. Two of them lumbered into view before coming to a sudden halt. The reason for their sudden stop was in the shape of Sophia's Glock-19 held in a two-handed grip and pointed right at them. 'I have nineteen rounds. Even if I was half- cut I'm going to get one of you. And for the record, I'm not half-cut.' The men looked at each other. It was an instinctive action, but with the tinted visors on their protective headgear a pointless exercise. 'Take your helmets off and get on your knees,' Sophia said. The men obeyed her with alacrity. She fished out a handful of heavy-duty plastic cable ties from her pocket. They'd saved her bacon on many occasions when she'd been caught up in a closing time brawl outside a beer cellar with a load of drunks. 'On your feet.' The men got up, never taking their eyes off the Glock. 'Over there.' She indicated towards where the other man was cuffed to the stack of castings.

The men shuffled over to the man and looked to her for further instructions. 'Sit down, hands behind your backs,' she nodded to Kurt. 'Fasten their hands together, then make a link round the cast with the other ties.' Kurt moved over to the men and soon had them trussed up. Three sets of eyes glared at them with uncontrolled hatred, and a dash of fear thrown in for good measure. Sophia picked up their helmets and jammed them over their heads back to front, making them effectively blind.

The whole operation had taken less than five minutes, but Sophia knew instinctively it had taken too long. Kurt had just started back to join her when the giant appeared in front of them. He was flanked by two men, each of whom carried guns held clumsily in their gloved hands.

'Drop the gun,' the giant's voice echoed out from behind his visor. Sophia raised her hands slowly in the air, edging backwards until she felt the cold weight of the gas cylinders pressing into her back. 'Put the gun down,' the giant said again.

Sophia slowly lowered her gun down with one hand, while her other hand was busy behind her. She suddenly ducked down, dragging Kurt to the floor with her. There was an explosive roar and a cloud of freezing CO_2 gas enveloped the giant and his two minions.

Their visors were instantly covered in a thick film of ice, effectively blinding them.'Run!' Sophia shouted, but Kurt was already moving as fast as his legs would carry him. Together they sprinted past the furnace and headed for the main entrance. And they nearly made it.

There were four of them. They must have been part of the security detail they'd missed seeing when they'd first arrived. They weren't wearing protective clothing, but what they did have were guns, and unlike the foundry workers it looked like they knew how to use them.

Sophia turned to Kurt, 'I think we may have reached a new low.' Kurt nodded. He could tell Sophia was giving him some sort of coded signal, and he'd discover what it was pretty soon.

'Put your gun down and get on the floor.''Better do as they say,' Sophia said, as she dropped her Glock. They both hit the ground as one. The Glock landed in the slag trough a millisecond later.

The security men froze. It was a rabbit in the head-lights moment. But not for long. As the bullets cooked off they exploded, piercing the dark like a swarm of lightning bugs. The men ran for cover as pieces of red-hot metal ricocheted around them.

One of the men clutched his ear and howled in pain as a piece of shrapnel hit the side of his head. 'Motherfucker,' he slapped at his damaged ear and tried to massage the pain away. The munitions gave their last snap, crackle and pop and the men regrouped. Sophia and Kurt stood up. Sophia sensed him before they saw him, his body odour preceding his arrival. She felt the cold rim of his gun pressing into her neck, and his hot rancid breath as he leant down and spoke to her. 'Don't make a fucking move.'

CHAPTER THIRTY-SIX

Sophia tested the ropes cutting into her wrists and ankles. It was a futile exercise. They were taut enough to cut off the circulation and she could already feel a numbness in her fingers as the blood flow slowed. She looked across at Kurt and saw the terror in his eyes. Looming over them was a vast wall of rusty pipes and cables that surrounded the monstrous blast furnace radiating heat from the molten steel within its white-hot belly.

The orange glow spilling from its throat bathed the foundries darkness in a blood-red glow. Like actors in some post-apocalyptic sci-fi movie, figures dressed in silver heat retardant suits and protective helmets moved slowly around the vast industrial building that housed the furnace. She twisted her head and tried to look around. She could make out some men unloading gold bars from the back of a truck onto a forklift at one end of the massive shed. In the gloom to one side of the furnace were a series of objects covered by heavy-duty tarpaulins.

She could understand if they were using the furnace to melt down stolen statues or metal items, but what were they doing with the gold?

All of these thoughts evaporated when two men dressed in protective clothing appeared beside her. Their opaque facemasks stared at her with unsettling blankness.

The taller of the two spoke disjointed English in a thick Russian accent. 'You cause us big trouble. We have to alter plans in case you tell others.'

Sophia shook her head. 'No one knows we're here.'

The big man shrugged. 'No matter. People come looking for you.'

'I'm a police officer. Untie us and there may be a chance you'll get a reduced sentence.' Sophia imagined the grim smile behind the Russians reflective mask.'Not possible. You like statues, maybe we make one for you.' A cold chill ran through Sophia. The knowledge that their operation involved the theft of statues did nothing to make her happy. It was what he was planning to do next that was worrying her. She looked at the man standing next to the Russian. He was holding a bucket of what looked like wet cement. The Russian pushed a tube into her mouth and did the same to Kurt. Sophia spat hers out. The Russian backhanded her.

'If you want to breathe keep it in.' He picked up the tube and Sophia opened her mouth and allowed him to slide it between her lips. The man with the bucket tipped it slowly over her head.

'Keep your eyes closed. Breathe through tube.'

Sophia shuddered as she felt the thick liquid slowly cover her face, her eyes, and her mouth. She gripped the tube with her teeth and took a shallow breath. Soon she was in darkness, and as the glutinous mixture filled her ears the noise of the foundry faded away. She felt the mixture start to harden and the pressure on her skin began to increase. A wave of panic began to sweep over her and she bit down harder on the breathing tube she'd fought against moments earlier. With her sight and hearing gone, all that was left for her to experience was the rough touch of their hands.

CHAPTER THIRTY-SEVEN

Hoog took a swig of strong coffee and headed up the galley steps to the deck of his barge. The sun was still only half awake, winking like some vast pink eyelid above the horizon, and this perfectly mirrored his condition. He'd drunk too much and stayed too long at Katja's flat and now he was paying the price.

He did a few cursory lunges to stretch his groin muscles and some running on the spot to warm his calves before setting off on his morning jog. He'd learned to his cost that just going for it wasn't a good look if you strained a hamstring. He headed down the path alongside the Coupure canal and made for the first windmill before looping round it and retracing his route. Once back home he would shower, change into his work clothes, down another coffee and head off.

He spotted the old man with the ancient terrier in the distance and gave a wave and a cheery greeting as he passed.

A gaggle of women sprinted towards him in a wave of brightly-coloured lycra, arguing volubly about some TV series they'd all seen. He gave them a mock salute as they passed.

As he approached the barge he saw his neighbor Koen Van Rikker watering his plants along the roof above his wheelhouse. He nodded to him as he did his cool down stretches. 'Up early this morning,' he said.

Koen smiled. 'Best time to water them if it's going to be sunny. That way you don't burn the leaves.'

'Sounds good,' Hoog said. He had no idea about how to treat flowers or shrubs, but had an ability to kill a pot plant at fifty paces. He finished his stretches and climbed onto his barge.

The sun was now clear of the horizon and the surface of the canal shimmered with diamonds of light. He climbed down the steps, went into the shower room, switched on the heater and ran the water. He tested the temperature before shrugging off his running gear and easing himself beneath the jets of water.

You had to have the reflexes of a cat and the suppleness of a snake to avoid concussion living in the cramped interior of a barge, and the more he thought about it the more he warmed to the idea of moving in with Katja.

He finished his shower, turned the water off and shimmied over to the heated rail. He grabbed a towel to dry himself off and was soon officially awake, and only one mug of coffee away from becoming a fully functioning human being. He changed into his work clothes and added some items into his rucksack. When the weather was good he always made a point of walking to the police station in Kartuizerinnenstraat.

He enjoyed moving amongst the flood of tourists and residents making their way on foot or bike into the ancient city centre. He found it grounded him, and gave him a sense of community.

Bruges had always had an uneasy relationship with tourists. The mayor had recently launched a wide-reaching campaign to try and control the number of cruise ships docking outside the city, and impose a system to stagger the timing of the guided tours on foot and in buses clogging up the narrow streets.

Husbanding the millions of tourist euros pouring into the city's coffers while appeasing the local residents had been an impossible balancing act. Hoog walked beside the Coupure canal towards the city centre until it became the Groenerei, and continued on to the old fish market.

Tourists were busy picking through the jewellery gloves, scarves and paintings on sale from the stall owners that took over from the fish sellers during the week. The man with the hand loom gave him a nod and a wave. With his facial recognition skills, he would have made a good police officer. Hoog had bought Katja a scarf from him recently, and like a dog never forgets where he's buried a bone this man never forgot a customer.

He cut through Blind Donkey street across the Dijver canal, past the City Hall and into the bustling square of the Burg, squeezing past the walking tours that already thronged the area. Moments later he was headed down Breidelstraat and into Woolestraat. He dodged a flock of Japanese tourists on Segways headed for the Belfort, and hurried down Oude Burg, taking a left into Kartuizerinnenstraat, squeezing past tourists queuing for the Bourgogne Des Flandres brewery tour.

Though one of his main hobbies was mastering various dance steps, he found dodging tourists on his way to work often involved deft footwork and a multitude of pirouettes. Seconds later he was outside the police station.

He headed through the glass doors and saw Ward behind the reception desk. This was strange as normally Sophia opted to take the late shift on Thursday night and a morning shift on Friday so she could have a longer weekend off. 'No Sophia?' Hoog asked.

Ward shrugged, 'No. I've rung her house and mobile,

just got the answer machine. Some officers have been round to her house but she's not in.'

Hoog leant forward. 'What was the last entry in the station log?'

Ward skimmed through the log and ran his figure down the page. 'Nothing until she signed out,' he held up a post-it note. 'This was on the monitor screen.'

'If I'm late in blame it on Hoog and his weird friend.' Hoog shook his head, 'What does she mean?' Ward asked.

Hoog smiled. 'I think she's talking about Kurt.'

'The conspiracy nut?' Ward said. 'I wouldn't say nut,' Hoog said. 'He's just on a different page than the rest of us.'

'More like a different planet,' Ward said.

Hoog turned to see Bakker being escorted up from the steps leading from the holding cells beneath the station. He didn't look happy.

'Problem?' Hoog asked.

Bakker nodded. 'I thought you promised me somewhere in Madeira, not bloody Menorca,' he said.

'No, you promised yourself Madeira, we promised to keep you safe. Once you've settled in, and answered any questions that might arise as a result of our investigation, then we can see if we can find you somewhere else to your liking...'

'Bloody Cala'n Porta, it's full of English tourists!'

Hoog was running out of patience, and getting worried about Sophia. 'We're a police force, not a travel agency. Besides, Madeira is full of hills, so you'll need to get a damn sight fitter before you move out there.' Hoog nodded to the officers and they took Bakker out of reception and into a waiting van outside.

Hoog pulled out his mobile and tapped a contact. He listened as the phone rang out.

'Hi, Kurt. It's Hoog. Just wondered if you have any idea where Sophia is? Call me back.'

He ended the call, unease starting to gnaw at him. 'What would she be doing with Kurt that would make her late for her shift?' Ward asked

Hoog shook his head. 'I don't know.''I think we should pay a visit to Kurt's place. It's not like Sophia to be late for her shift, maybe she's with him.'

Hoog had to agree. Sophia was the kind of officer that would turn up for her shift even if she had two broken legs. 'Okay, it won't take long, we'll head over there now.' As they headed for the exit Katja came through the door. One look at Hoog's face told her something was wrong.

'What's happening?''Sophia didn't turn up for her shift this morning. We think she's with Kurt.'

'You think he's kidnapped her?'

Hoog shook his head. 'No, we think she may have got involved with one of his conspiracies.

'What sort of conspiracy?' Katja asked.

'No idea. You know what he's like.'

'Yes. But it's not like Sophia to get sucked into one of his crazy stories. What are you going to do? I assume you've tried ringing them?'

Hoog nodded. 'Yes. Both mobiles went to voicemail and no one's picking up their landlines. We're going to go over to Kurt's place and see if we can get any clues as to where they might be.'

'Maybe you can track down their mobiles,' Katja said, looking at Ward.

He nodded. 'I'll give it a go.'

'Okay,' Hoog said.

They headed out of the main entrance and down to the car pool. Hoog looked around and his eyes fastened on two brand new Model X Tesla's parked in the corner of the pound. They sat there, their paintwork gleaming in the morning sunshine.

Katja gave Hoog a look. 'You are joking,' she said.

Hoog smiled. 'I know what you're thinking. You're thinking I shouldn't risk smashing up another expensive car so soon after the last one.'

Katja shook her head. 'Smashing is an understatement to describe what happened to that Tesla. And it doesn't take a genius to work out that repeating the performance wouldn't be a good idea.'

Hoog wagged a finger. 'Look at it from an environmental point of view. It's electric, less pollution and less noise.'

Katja sighed. Once Hoog had an idea in his head it was impossible to shift him. 'Okay, let's not waste any more time talking about saving the planet when we should be finding Sophia and Kurt. Assuming they want to be found.'

Hoog smiled and fished out his mobile. He placed his finger on the screen and the nearest Tesla gave a muted click as the engine started up with a low purr. The falcon wing doors arched open and Ward slid into the back seat clutching his rucksack and laptop. Hoog climbed behind the wheel and Katja got into the passenger seat.

They were soon humming through the city headed for the ring road. Hoog joined the slip road leading onto the R30 and floored the accelerator. He activated the siren and lights and the traffic shrank into the slow lane. Moments later they were headed towards the Gentpoort City Gate.

Compared to their recent experience the trip seemed quite sedate. The gate was soon visible in the distance and Hoog began to slow.

'I rang the museum curator and he'll be there to let us into Kurt's apartment,' he said. 'He may be in. We don't know why he didn't pick up. It could be for a variety of reasons. It wouldn't be the first time a mobile network has gone down,' Katja said.

Ward looked up from his laptop in the back. 'It's a bit of a coincidence that they're both down. I'll try and trace their mobiles again. As long as their batteries aren't flat I might be able to hack into them.'

'How can you do that if they're switched off,' Katja asked.

Ward smiled, 'The NSA can crack your firmware or infect your phone with a Trojan virus so it looks like it's shutting down when you switch it off. Then they can force your phone to continue emitting a signal even if it's in standby mode. To be safe you'd need to remove the battery.'

'I'm sorry I asked.' Katja said.

Hoog turned off the ring road, drove across the Gentpoort bridge, past the broken barrier and parked at the side of the road with the hazard lights on.

'That's Sophia's car,' Hoog said, looking across at a small pink Fiat Panda at the side of the road. A short balding man wearing spectacles and a crumpled tweed jacket trotted towards them. He saw Hoog and thrust out a hand. 'Van Drug,' he said.

Hoog shook his hand. 'Thank you for your help.'

'No problem.'

They followed him as he pushed through the outer door of the museum entrance and headed up the narrow stone stairs. 'It's a bit tight in here,' he said.

They squeezed up the stairs and into the main floor

of the museum before walking across to another smaller door with a doorbell to one side. Van Drug pressed the button and there was the sound of a muted buzz behind the door. 'Just in case he's sleeping. He does keep strange hours sometimes. But I can't complain about his work ethic, he keeps the museum spotless.' Van Drug produced a key and opened the door. They followed him up another set of winding stone steps and were soon inside Kurt's cramped accommodation. 'I'll leave you to it,' Van Drug said, handing Hoog the keys.

Hoog took the keys and slipped them into his pocket. 'Thank you, we'll drop them back when we leave.' Van Drug nodded and scuttled back down the stairs. They were left staring at a large corkboard covered in pictures and diagrams.

Katja spoke first, 'I guess this is his latest conspiracy?'

CHAPTER THIRTY-EIGHT

Ward's fingers flew across the keys like a cricket rubbing its wings together. 'Both of their mobiles are back on,' he said.

'Is that down to you?' Katja said. Ward shook his head. 'I'd like to claim that, but I'd be lying,' he said.

Hoog and Katja looked over Ward's shoulder at the screen as the satellite image zoomed in on the coordinates of the two mobiles. The image stabilized and they were left looking at two overlapping, pulsing red blobs with GPS coordinates beneath them.

'They're both in the same area,' Hoog said. 'It looks like it,' Ward said. 'And it matches the address of the foundry Kurt was monitoring. Katja looked at the screen and back to the corkboard. 'Maldegem.' She turned to see Hoog already headed for the door.

Hoog accelerated across the bridge and hung a left onto the ring road, leaving a trail of rubber behind. With the blue light on and the siren in full voice, Hoog selected *Ludicrous-Plus* mode and crushed the accelerator beneath his foot. Within half an hour Hoog was pulling off the R30 and onto the N9 motorway heading for Maldegem.

'Well that wasn't dangerous,' Katja said, releasing her grip from the overhead grab handle and shaking her hand to get some feeling back into it.

Hoog shot her a look. 'You can never get to a scene too early,' Hoog snorted. 'Or a funeral,' Katja said. They continued along the N9 for ten minutes before peeling off at the Maldegem junction. Hoog killed the siren and left the blue light on as they cut through the town centre and followed the signs towards the industrial estate on the outskirts of the town. They drove past deserted warehouses and offices until Katja saw something in the distance.'There it is,' Katja said, pointing towards a large warehouse on the edge of the estate.

Hoog headed towards the site until he saw a small car park nearby. He nodded at the car park.'That's Kurt's car,' he said, pointing at the classic Volvo. 'Why am I not surprised?' Katja said. Hoog swung into the car park and switched the engine off. They climbed out of the Tesla and Hoog un-holstered his gun.'Should I call for back-up?' Katja asked.

Hoog shook his head. 'Let's take a look at the situation first.'

Katja and Ward un-holstered their guns and followed Hoog.

Hoog reached a small metal door set into the large sliding door that formed the main entrance to the foundry. He held up his hand in the standard holding signal and Ward and Katja came to a halt. He reached down and slowly turned the handle. The door opened and Hoog slipped through. Ward and Katja followed.

They stood with their backs to the door and looked around. The acrid smell of molten metal filled their nostrils, and a veil of smoke hung in the air. Hoog pulled out a torch and levelled it along his raised gun, sweeping the area. The only sources of light were the dull glow from the furnace and an orange light leaking from the transfer ladle that hung from the overhead gantry crane.

Ward and Katja added their torches to the gloom.

Hoog called out, 'Police! Come out with your hands up.' His voice reverberated off the hard metal surfaces surrounding them. Hoog's torch swept over the foundry floor and halted. 'What is it?' Katja said, angling her beam towards Hoog's.

Ward swung his torch until it joined the others, lighting up the object in a wash of light. It was a statue.

They moved slowly towards it, alert to the slightest sound. But other than the crackle of cooling metal, the foundry remained silent. They reached the statue and stood in front of it. It was a nude study of two lovers, a man and a woman. But these were lovers with a difference. Hoog reached out to the pendant that hung from the woman's neck. It was a silver St Christopher pendant, the one he'd last seen around Sophia's neck.

He looked at the man. On his finger was a familiar signet ring. The CIA one he'd last seen on Kurt's finger.

'Jesus,' Hoog said.

Katja shook her head. 'I don't understand.' The faces of the man and the woman were all too familiar. They were Sophia and Kurt. Katja laid her hand on Sophia's neck. 'Still warm.'

Hoog walked behind the statue. Both of them had a mobile phone taped to their backs. There was also some kind of breathing tube hanging down behind their necks. Hoog's foot slid on something, and he clutched onto the statue to keep from falling.

He pointed his torch at the floor. Behind each of the statues a pool of blood glittered in the light. To his mind the blood could only belong to two people, Sophia and Kurt. If that wasn't terrifying enough, what he imagined had been done to them was infinitely worse.

CHAPTER THIRTY-NINE

Kruger the coroner listened through his stethoscope and shook his head. 'Nothing. That doesn't mean much as I'm listening through a bronze mask.' Behind him a technician was using an e-sniffer, an ultra-high-speed gas chromatography device with an LCD display and a probe on a flexible lead. He held the probe next to the two breathing tubes that hung out of the back of each of the bronze heads and checked the readings on the screen.

'Traces of carbon dioxide on both tubes. I would say they've been recently used.' 'What about the blood?' Hoog asked, rubbing his face. A female technician was studying the screen on a small handheld device. 'Not so long ago you'd have had to wait hours if not days to get any DNA. Isn't that right Jenny?' Kruger said.

Jenny looked up from the screen. 'You're right. But this has a molecular chip. It's connected through the cloud to all the available databases. We can check a sample within fifteen minutes,' she looked at her watch. 'Not long now,' she said.

Hoog had been checking his watch like a nervous tic since they'd started the procedure and the technicians went through their routines. Jenny's device gave out a muted ping. 'Got it!' Jenny said.'Two hits on the database. It's Sophia and Kurt.' Dread knotted Hoog's stomach. The odds of their survival had drastically shortened with each new piece of evidence. A man came over holding a circular saw with a carbide blade. 'What do you want me to do?' he asked.

Hoog looked at Katja and Ward, and rubbed his face nervously again. If what he imagined was true, then Sophia and Kurt were already dead. Whoever had done this to them didn't care if they lived or died. They were just sending a grim message. There had been no tip off, no gloating message posted on social media. Two people he cared about had been deliberately murdered in cold blood, in the most horrific way imaginable.

He looked at the bronze faces of Sophia and Kurt. The likeness was astonishing. They could only have been cast while they were still alive. But if there was a chance they could be saved he had to take it. He nodded to the man with the saw. 'Do it,' Hoog said. He turned away as the blade screamed against the metal of Sophia's neck.

A shower of sparks waterfalled to the ground as the man cut deeper into the metal. Sophia's head hung at a drunken angle and the man cut the power. Hoog forced himself to look. The statue was hollow. There was a sheet of paper inside the neck.

'They wanted us to think they'd made Sophia and Kurt into living statues, to scare the hell out of us, send a message,' Ward said.

Hoog swore, 'Bastards. I'll send them a bloody message.' He carefully removed the piece of paper. Read the message scrawled on it. *'Try to follow us and their next death will be real.'*

Hoog shook his head. 'They could just kill them anyway and we'd never know. The sooner we get after them the more chance we have of finding them alive.'

Ward and Katja nodded. 'I agree. What do you want to do?' Katja asked. 'Let the SOCOs do their work. Looks like they packed up in a hurry, so there's a chance they may have left some clues behind,' Hoog said.

Katja gave Hoog's arm a squeeze. 'We'll find them. Even if we have to write off another Tesla.' Hoog gave a grim smile.

'Or two,' he said.

CHAPTER FORTY

It was cold and dark, and the smell of oil and petrol filled her nostrils.

'Are you okay?' Kurt's voice echoed around the metal container. Sophia shook her head. She'd been drugged with something that had left a metallic taste in her mouth along with a splitting headache.'I'm fine,' she lied. 'You're as bad a liar as I am a fighter,' Kurt said.

'You're right. I feel like shit. Where are we?' '

'Just a minute.' She heard Kurt shifting around and then a beam of light blinded her. 'Sorry,' Kurt said. 'Where did you stash that?' Sophia asked.

One of the last things she remembered was going through a rough search, so she had no idea how Kurt had managed to hide anything.

'I am a prepper,' Kurt said. He played the beam of

the torch around the dark space and then back to one of his shoes. He fiddled with the heel and produced a small multi-tool. 'You really are Inspector Gadget,' Sophia said.

'It's not a lock pick, but it's better than nothing,' Kurt said. He swung the torch around their prison.

Sophia saw a small car in front of heavy duty metal doors. They were inside some kind of a freight container on the back of a truck.'How long have I been out?' Sophia asked. 'About an hour,' Kurt said.

Sophia nodded. 'We need to get out of here.'

'I'm with you on that. But we might need to wait until we get to where we're going. This container is a bit of a steel coffin even if we weren't both cuffed.'

Sophia looked down at her hand. Her captors had used her cuffs to connect them both to some immovable metal object under a tarpaulin at the back of the container.

'Can you stand up?' she asked. 'I want to take a look at what's under here.'

Kurt nodded and they carefully stood up in sync. The tarpaulin slid up as they stood, and Kurt played the beam over the dark bronze shape of the statue's leg they were cuffed to. Kurt pointed the torch upwards under the tarpaulin. He recognised what it was immediately.

'It's the 't Zand Square statue,' he said. 'They must be shipping it out of the country. We messed up their plans.

They must be taking it somewhere else before melting it down.'

She nodded towards the car. 'What's that?

Kurt smiled. 'It's a 1965 classic Mini MK 1 Cooper S, 1275cc engine. Worth about 50,000 euros these days. It probably has twin 1.25" SU carburetors. The roof's painted red and white, which were the colours of Paddy Hopkirks Monte Carlo winning rally car. With a high-performance cylinder head and a straight through exhaust you're looking at over 80 horsepower at 5800 rpm.' He paused. Sophia looked at him, shaking her head.

'At a guess,' he said with a smile.

'You really are a petrol head aren't you.' Sophia said.

Kurt grinned. 'My dad had one just like this back in the day. He was constantly tuning it. Skimming the cylinder head. Fitting high performance valves, tuning the carbs. I used to bring him cups of tea and watch him work,' Kurt said.

'Did you ever see a film with Michael Caine called The Italian Job? Not the modern remake but the original.'

Sophia shook her head. 'Wasn't he the English guy who played Batman's butler?' she said.

'Okay, your ignorance is forgiven because you're not a man in his seventies. The film involved a load of Minis pulling stunts and racing through the streets of Turin, and a sewer pipe. After the film was released every teenager on the planet wanted a Mini.'

Sophia nodded. 'So, this Classic is being delivered to a rich collector somewhere. And as we don't have any food and water I'm guessing they can't be too far away.'

'Or they don't care if we live or die,' Kurt said.

'Thanks, Captain Buzzkill. What other tools do you have in your Inspector Gadget kit?'

Kurt fiddled with the multi-tool and opened up various parts of it. 'Bottle opener, cross hatch screwdriver, flat head, knife, mini-saw, file and a spike...though that could be a tool for getting stones out of horse's hooves.'

'That might be more useful back in Bruges,' Sophia said.

'Let me look at it,' she waited while he angled the torch and pried open the small spike from the side of the tool. She looked at it. 'I could probably use it as a pick. Handcuffs aren't that sophisticated. Give it to me.' Kurt handed it to her. 'Keep your hand still.' Kurt held his hand out with the cuff on and Sophia used her free hand and the knife's spike to ease into the handcuff lock on Kurt's cuff. 'Have you done this before?' he asked.

Sophia didn't look at him or relax her concentration. 'Once. I was a lot younger and it was very embarrassing.'

Kurt smiled. 'I won't mention it again.' There was a

click and he felt the cuff fall away from his wrist. Kurt smiled. 'Good job.'

Sophia pulled the cuffs clear from behind the statue. She fiddled with the cuff on her wrist and was soon free. She stood up and shook her wrists, getting the circulation back.'Shine the torch towards the car.' Kurt played the beam over the Mini. Sophia went over to the door and pressed the button on the handle. There was a click and the door swung open.

'I guess they don't need to worry about security inside a locked container.' Sophia fumbled around the miniscule dashboard. Kurt came over.'Let me. They've even left the key in the ignition.' Kurt turned the ignition key and flicked a switch. The headlamps came on and a wash of light bounced off the rear door of the container, showing them their surroundings in grim detail. 'If you want main beam you use your foot to press the metal button on the floor.' Kurt climbed into the driving seat and activated the switch with his foot. The lights dipped off and on.

'That's weird, but oddly sensible,' Sophia said. 'Save the lights in case we flatten the battery.'

Kurt flicked a switch that just left the sidelights on. 'If they are planning to starve us to death, I think I'd prefer carbon monoxide poisoning.'

'I don't want to go down that road. We're getting out of here, I can promise you that.' She slid into the passenger seat and looked around the sparse cabin. 'No car alarm, key fob, or remote boot release.'

'Welcome to my world,' Kurt said.

'At least we don't have to hot wire it.'

Kurt looked at her. 'Planning on going for a drive?'

Sophia shrugged. 'Might be an option.'

'Sure, all we have to do is get out of a locked shipping container and past a bunch of murderous Russians and we're home free.'

Sophia reached up to the sun visor above the passenger seat. There was a bunch of folded documents wedged there. She pulled them down and flicked through them. 'What are they?' Kurt asked.

Sophia studied them. 'Shipping documents.'

'Does it say where we're headed?'

'Antwerp, and then on to St Petersburg.'

Sophia looked at the arrival dates. It wasn't good news. 'Shit, that's nine days.'

Kurt looked over at the documents. 'My geography's not great, but that route doesn't make much sense. They'd be going the long way around Denmark, and under that amazing bridge, the one they used in the drama series.'

Sophia nodded. She'd been a big fan of The Bridge. 'The Øresund Bridge.' 'Yes, that's it,' Kurt said, 'It would make more sense to drive to Hamburg then continue on by sea.' 'Maybe they're using the route with the least security.'

'St Petersburg is where the ship docks, not our final destination. We don't know how far they're going once they've unloaded the container.' The truck lurched and began to slow down. Kurt looked at his watch. 'We must be getting near the terminal.' Sophia racked her brains. 'We probably have about an hour before loading.' 'Turn the lights off,' Sophia said. 'What is it?' Kurt asked as he flicked the light switch off, plunging them into darkness.

'I'm just waiting for my eyes to adjust,' Sophia said. There was the muted sound of heavy doors opening and closing and voices. Sophia looked towards the back door. She saw a faint glow of light leaking between the top and bottom of the doors. She opened the passenger door and looked up. A glimmer of daylight was spilling from a vent in the container's roof.

'We won't die of suffocation. I'm guessing they needed ventilation to disperse any fumes from the car's fuel tank,' Sophia said.

'So, the worst-case scenario is we starve to death,' Kurt said. Sophia shook her head. 'No, we're getting out of here.' 'How?' Kurt asked. 'Give me a moment, I haven't worked out all the details yet.'

Kurt shook his head. 'Right, I'm guessing you haven't actually got a plan then.'

'Not quite,' Sophia said with a smile.

'No problem, nice try at keeping my spirits up though,' Kurt said.

'I'd be really upset if you didn't get to solve your latest big conspiracy.'

'Don't worry about it. If I hadn't pestered you to get involved we wouldn't be stuck in a shipping container on our way to Russia,' Kurt said.

'Still...' Sophia trailed off.

Kurt smiled and shook his head. 'I've spent too long living inside my conspiracy bubble. I've lived more life in the last twelve hours than I've had in years. And that's all down to you.'

Sophia thought about that. It wasn't strictly true. After all, he'd tried to help the homeless when they needed it most.

'You've lived outside your head on a few occasions. You helped the homeless...'

'And pissed off the police,' Kurt grinned.

'Well, Hoog didn't seem to think so.'

'Hoog's his own man, and for a detective he has more in common with me than he cares to admit.

Sophia smiled. 'He's certainly his own man, that's for sure. If he didn't have such a high case clear-up rate he'd be on the street issuing parking tickets by now.' They shared a moment of silence. Sophia broke it. 'Okay. If we have any chance of breaking out of here we have to do it at the right time.' 'If we break out too early and the driver sees us, we could wind up dead,' Kurt said. 'For sure. Once we've been through security the next stop is loading.'

Kurt looked at her.'Okay. So how do you intend to break out?'

Sophia smiled at him. 'You're not going to like it.'

CHAPTER FORTY-ONE

Hanna picked up the large, wooden- framed picture and lugged it across the floor before placing it next to a collection of six more paintings leaning against the wall in a corner of the storeroom. They were still awaiting classification and Erika had asked her to make a bit of space for some new arrivals. She looked around the cavernous space and relished her good fortune in landing the assistant's job helping Erika.

Being surrounded by such a wealth of history and art had been a dream come true. Erika was also a wealth of historical information, and during the quiet times in the museum she loved sharing a cup of coffee and listening to her exploits, learning of the history surrounding the various Dutch Masters on display.

She went over to another group of paintings and

moved one of them to a new home on the far wall. As she leant to put it down, it slipped through her hands, catching her palm with a rough edge.

'Shit!' she yelped, putting the picture down and rubbing at the palm of her hand.

Erika appeared at the doorway. 'Are you all right?' she asked.

Hanna sucked at the palm of her hand. I'm fine, damn splinters,' she said.

Erika looked at her strangely. 'Splinters?'

Hanna stared at Erika. 'Yes why, are you okay?'

Erika smiled. 'I'm more than okay,' she said, before repeating the word again, her smile broadening. 'Splinters. You just reminded me of the name of the Russian organization my businessman friend told me about.'

'The organization controlling the amount of gold in circulation?' Hanna asked.

'Yes. In Russian it was Plintus, but in English it's Plinth,' Erika said, smiling at Hanna.

I'll let Hoog know, it could be important.'

Erika took Hanna's hand and looked at it.

'I have a pair of tweezers and a magnifying glass upstairs, let's get that splinter out of your hand before it goes septic.'

CHAPTER FORTY-TWO

Hoog stood in the foundry, sipping a cup of coffee and chewing on a biscuit. SOCO's were crawling all over the area. Kruger, the coroner, came over to join them. Even though he didn't have a victim to deal with, he'd insisted on staying. He'd known Sophia for as long as Hoog and if there was the slightest chance of finding a clue that might save her and Kurt he wanted to help find it. 'They certainly wanted to scare the crap out of you,' he announced jovially. 'That's for sure,' Hoog said. And thanks for the coffee and biscuits by the way.'

'No sweat, I know you're a sugar addict.' Hoog smiled and took another sip of coffee before speaking. 'I've always said you have remarkable powers of deduction.'

Kruger grunted. 'I won't disagree with that,' he said, looking at the headless statue.

'They used plaster of Paris to form the original mould, and gave Sophia and Kurt breathing tubes while the plaster hardened. It's not pleasant, but at least you can breathe. Once it set they would have split the casts down the side and removed them from their faces. Then they joined the two halves again and poured wax into the plaster mould. Once that set, they coated the wax with a ceramic mix which then formed the receptacle for the molten bronze which melts the wax which is drained away, or lost...'

'The lost wax process...' Katja said.

'I'm impressed,' Kruger said.

'Then they welded the heads onto the original statue of the lovers, leaving the breathing tubes, the pendant, the ring and some blood to complete the effect,' Katja said.

Hoog nodded. 'They wanted to show us how ruthless they could be if we got in their way,' Hoog said.

'We've found traces of bronze, gold, and ammonium sulphide in the transfer ladle.' Hoog looked at him. Kruger gestured towards the gantry crane above. 'That big bucket hanging from the gantry crane?'

Hoog remembered back to the crates of chemicals they'd found in Bakker's antique shop in Predikherenstraat. Ammonium sulphide had been one of them.

'What's ammonium sulphide used for?' Hoog asked.

'It ages the bronze, gives it a blue-black patina.'

'Why do you think they were using that?' Hoog asked.

Kruger shrugged. 'That's one of many unanswered questions right now.' Katja came over with some printouts. 'Found something?'

Katja nodded at Hoog. 'The CCTV inside was shut down, but I managed to get some information from the weighing machine. The trucks coming in are automatically weighed, time-stamped and image captured. All of the data is stored in the cloud and on their servers. Ward managed to download the most recent files.'

Hoog studied the printouts. There was a shot of the front of a Dennison truck and the driver. 'Let's see if this low-life is in any of our databases,' Hoog said.'Ward's already on it. Nothing so far,' Katja said.

Hoog flicked through another printout, showing a picture of a classic Mini-1275 Cooper S, the driver's face obscured by the sun visor. 'Any sign of this car?' Hoog asked.'I'm coming to that,' Katja said. She showed Hoog a picture of the Dennison truck leaving the foundry. 'This is it fully loaded and shows the truck leaving before we arrived,' she tapped some figures on another printout. 'The truck coming in weighs 7750k, which includes the driver, but when it leaves it weighs 13531k, a difference of 5781k.'

Hoog looked at the figures. 'The Mini clocked in at 650k, and if Kurt's conspiracy is a reality and the t'Zand statue is in the truck, we can add 5000k.'

'That leaves 131kilos unaccounted for,' Katja said.

Hoog slapped his hand on a steel girder, making a sharp crack. 'Damn! Those bastards have got Sophia and Kurt in that container.'

Ward came over holding a printout. 'I managed to get this from the printer memory.'

'What is it?' Hoog asked.

'It's a copy of the bill of lading. Leaving from Antwerp with a final destination of St Petersburg,' Ward said.

'We need to put out an APB to all police and border control security at Antwerp, and check any trucks heading for the port,' Hoog said.

Ward opened his laptop. 'I managed to get some CCTV from the car park opposite the foundry. One of them has the main entrance in the background.' He tapped the tracker pad. A video clip played. They watched as a heavily loaded container truck reversed out of the foundry.

'What's the time stamp on that?' Hoog asked.

Ward looked at the screen. 'An hour ago. We just missed them.'

Hoog swallowed the last mouthful of coffee and bit into a biscuit. 'Not yet we haven't. C'mon.' Katja and

Ward jogged after Hoog as he headed towards the car park.

'Good luck,' Konrad called after them.

The Tesla was already headed towards them by the time they reached the car park entrance. The falcon wing doors swung up and Ward scrambled into the back as Hoog and Katja climbed in through the front doors. They fastened their seatbelts and Hoog sent the Tesla rocketing through the open barrier.

'Border control will be on the lookout for those plates, but there's a chance they could be switched before they get to the port,' Ward said. 'I'll access CCTV and traffic cameras on the route and see if I can pick anything up.'

Katja turned to Hoog. 'How do you deal with the digital emasculation of today's police force?'

'What do you mean?' Hoog said.

'I mean with the thousands of CCTV cameras, along with the digital footprints left for the cybercrime force, it only leaves you with the brute force side of things. The punching, shooting, and car chases.'

Hoog smiled. 'What's not to like?' Hoog said.

'Maybe in your case you enjoy the more hands-on approach to policing,' Katja said.

'Well, I don't miss the hours of tedious door-to-door investigation and the endless searching through files in the archives. That's for sure,' Hoog said.

'So I suppose it's a bit of a Yin and Yang situation between you and the geek squad,' Katja said.

'We play to our strengths. I ask Ward for the impossible and in exchange for that I make sure the bad guys he helps track down don't slip through our fingers,' Hoog said, flicking a look back at Ward. 'And I'm asking for the impossible right now, because if we can't track them down before they're loaded we may never find them,' he said, switching on the siren and pressing the accelerator to the floor.

CHAPTER FORTY-THREE

Kurt looked at his watch. 'We haven't got much time.'

Sophia nodded. 'There's always a chance that border control will want to inspect the cargo.'

'I'm guessing they'll have no problem killing us ahead of schedule if we try to alert them,' Kurt said. Sophia thought about this. They'd had ample chance to kill them and yet they'd taken the risk of keeping them alive. There was only one reason that made any sense. 'They must have left a message behind at the foundry. Some kind of threat to our lives if anybody came after us,' Sophia said.'That's assuming Hoog was able to track down the foundry where we were held.'

'Maybe they made sure he did. They took both of

our mobiles after all; they could have turned them on so they could be tracked. Also, once Hoog and Katja realised we were both missing they would have gone to your place. I'm sure there was enough information there for Ward to work out where we were headed,' Sophia said.

Kurt looked at her. 'You're right. They only have to slow them down until the container's loaded and on its way, and they're home free.'

Sophia thought about that. She was confident that Hoog and his team would know the risks associated with tracking them down and mounting a rescue mission.

'There's only one time we can risk drawing attention to ourselves, and that's when the crane loads our container onto the ship. At that point there will be enough people in the area to halt the loading procedure if they notice something suspicious. And once they check inside the container we're out of here.'

Sophia paused. 'If we get this wrong we're all out of options. Once we're stacked on the deck we'll be boxed in, top, bottom and sides.'

The more she thought about it the more convinced she was that her plan was the only chance they had. She could feel the truck inching forward. She looked at Kurt.'So, what do you really think's going on here?' Sophia asked.

'I think Russia, the state, or a Russian OCG are involved, and it might even be a combination of the two,' Kurt said.

'You think they're using organised crime gangs to carry out their agenda?' Sophia asked.

'Yes, with plausible deniability of course.'

'Go on,' Sophia said.

'First of all, it involves the theft of statues on a global scale.'

'Right, and then they resurface weeks, or months later.'

'Yes,' Kurt said.

'Except in this case we're headed to Russia with five tons of 't Zand statue.' Kurt flashed her a smile.

'I was wondering when you'd spot the yawning chasm in my conspiracy theory.'

'It is quite a sizeable hole.'

'I have a theory about that,' Kurt said.

'I'm all ears,' Sophia said.

'I still don't know why they're stealing and returning the statues, but in this instance, I think the gang involved decided to follow their own agenda.'

'So instead of returning the statue to its original home, they're taking it out of the country. But why risk changing the agenda?' Sophia asked.

'I'm not sure, but it could be to do with the gold we

saw in the foundry.' Sophia thought back to the crate of gold they'd seen in the fork lift truck.

'Maybe they've stolen the gold, and the statue. There could even be another container with the gold in it,' Sophia said.

'That's a bit risky isn't it? Kurt said.

'Yes. It's not something you could explain away too easily to customs. I saw a case file on Hoog's desk. One of the men he arrested was a commercial diver and they think he may have been involved in recovering the gold from a sunken WW1 U-boat off the coast of Oostende.'

'I read about the U-boat when they first discovered it. They designated it as a war grave,'

Sophia paused. She could hear the sound of trucks and men shouting getting louder. 'So, what's the connection between the gold, reappearing stolen statues, and reactivated foundries?'

Kurt shook his head, 'That's the billion euro question.' He opened the driver's door, stepped out and shone his torch towards the tarpaulin-covered statue at the back of the container. Something glittered in its beam.

Sophia rolled down her window. 'What is it?'

'I don't know,' Kurt said. Sophia opened the passenger door and followed him. Kurt walked over to the tarpaulin, lifted it up, and shone his torch down to where their handcuffs had cut into the dull bronze metal, exposing the layer below. They stared at the bright yellow metal glinting in the torchlight. 'Is that what I think it is?' Sophia asked. Kurt nodded. 'I'm not a metallurgist, but I'd say that was gold.'

CHAPTER FORTY-FOUR

The Tesla accelerated down the N9 and was soon joining the N49 headed for Antwerp. The wailing siren and flashing lights cleared a path through the traffic ahead of them. Hoog glanced at the time in the corner of the Tesla's large dashboard display screen. 'Any news?' he said.

Ward checked his laptop. 'They've sent me CCTV coverage up to the motorway and some traffic camera footage. They tracked the container truck leaving the E34 outside Antwerp.' Hoog blasted his horn at a car blocking his path and it swerved into the slow lane.

'Where's the truck now?' Hoog said.'They think it may have switched plates, as it was stationary an hour ago before we lost track of that particular license number.'

Hoog thumped the wheel in frustration. 'Dammit! What about the container truck itself? Didn't that have any form of physical identifying marks.'

Ward stared at the screen, fingers scampering across the tracker pad. 'We have the initial CCTV of the truck from outside the foundry, which has some markings on it, but they haven't spotted any of those on a truck yet. There's a chance they could have oversprayed them as well.'

'What about telematics or GPS tracking? I thought they all had tachographs linked to the cloud these days. The company that owns the truck must know exactly where they are 24/7 don't they?' Katja said.

Ward shrugged. 'That was the first thing I checked, and if it was a legitimate company we would have that information.'

Katja nodded, 'I'm guessing they're not legit?'

'No. The truck is registered through multiple shell companies in different countries all over the world. It could take weeks to unravel,' Ward said.

Hoog shook his head. 'C'mon, are you deaf and blind,' he yelled at a sluggish car in front of him, before continuing, 'So, we don't have any way of identifying the container other than visually?'

'I'm afraid not,' Ward said. 'But once we get to the port we'll have a better chance of finding it. If all the other trucks are registered through normal channels then we should be able to cross them off the list and narrow the search down for our man.'

'We don't have that much time,' Katja said.

Ward reached into his rucksack and produced a small circular device. 'I have something that might speed things up.' 'A drone?' Katja said. 'Yes.' Ward put it on the seat beside him. 'It's not as fast as the Tesla but it will be our eye in the sky once we get to the port.' Katja smiled, 'I remember the last time we used a drone.' Her mind flashed back to the underground canal beneath the Jan Van Eyck square and their deadly confrontation with a gang of armed thugs. 'I'm hoping this one will end up in better shape than the last one,' Ward said with a smile. 'Well at least no one will be shooting at this one.' Hoog glanced at Ward in the rearview mirror.

'I wouldn't bet on it.'

Ward looked at his screen. 'Border patrol have been instructed to flag up any suspect trucks, but not to conduct extra internal checks in case they alert the driver. We have to assume that Sophia and Kurt are still alive, and we don't want to put them at risk,' Ward said.

'Their message was pretty explicit,' Katja said.

Hoog cut the siren, switched off the flashing lights and eased back on the accelerator. 'Okay, the port's up ahead.' They wound their way round the circuitous entry to the loading area for trucks and halted at the barrier. A police officer came over to the car. Hoog buzzed the window down and showed his warrant card. The officer nodded. 'Detective Hoog. We've been expecting you. We're running visual checks to try and isolate the container. Nothing suspicious has been flagged up yet.' He handed Hoog a walkie-talkie. 'Officer Van de Brill is running the operation, on Channel one, and Jan Van Cleef, the port logistics officer is on Channel two.'

Hoog took the unit and stashed it in a pocket. 'Thank you.' The officer waved them through. Ward handed Katja the small drone. 'What do I do with it?'

'Just open the window and drop it.' 'Drop it?' Katja said, holding the device gingerly in the palm of her hand.

'Yes, like a bat,' Ward said.

'A bat?' Katja shook her head. Nonplussed.

'Bats can't take off from the ground, that's why they hang upside down; that way they can swoop up using their downwards momentum,' Ward said.

'That's good to know. Next time I find a bat on the ground I'll know what to do,' Katja said.

'Glad to hear it. The drone has an inertia trigger device that activates the motors as soon as it senses downwards momentum.' Katja buzzed the window down and carefully held the drone out. She closed her eyes and let it go. A millisecond later she watched as it shot up past her window, its four miniature rotor blades shrieking.

Wards fingers skimmed the tracker pad. 'I've blue

toothed it to the Tesla display. If we spot anything that looks suspicious we can relay it to the port authorities and they can slow the truck down until we get there.' The Tesla display filled with an overhead view of the port and lines of trucks streaming towards trains and container ships moored at the harbour. Hoog moved across into the truck lane.

'We have to find them before they reach the loading area,' Hoog said, banging the steering wheel in frustration.

CHAPTER FORTY-FIVE

'Really?' Kurt looked at Sophia, a look of disbelief on his face.

Sophia nodded. 'Unless you can think of another way.' They sat in front of the Mini, staring at the heavy steel doors that lay between them and freedom. 'No chance of picking the locks?' Kurt asked.

'All the locking mechanisms are on the outside of the container doors. There's no way out of here.' Kurt nodded. Much as it pained him to agree to Sophia's barbaric plan, the possibility of a slow death by starvation or worse was highly unappealing.'Okay, I need to check a few things,' he turned the ignition on, clambered out of the driver's seat and walked round to the boot. He rocked the car and listened. There was a muted whirr from some kind of motor. 'What's that noise?' Sophia asked. 'It's the fuel pump. If the fuel doesn't cover the lowest point in the tank when you rock the car it makes that sound. My father used to know exactly how low we were on fuel just by going round a corner.' He walked back to the bonnet and reached through the front of the grille. There was a click as he unlocked the catch and opened the bonnet.

He used a thin metal stay to prop it open. Seeing the diminutive engine compartment brought the memories flooding back.

His father had pointed out all of the major components to him when he was a boy. Brake fluid container, clutch fluid, cylinder head, SU Carburettor, accelerator cable, wiper motor...back then you could see everything. Not like the modern car engines where if you managed to get under the bonnet you were greeted by an amorphous lump of metal with zero sign of any components, and where getting a jump start needed a degree in mechanical engineering.

'Everything okay?' Sophia's voice snapped him out of his reverie.

He nodded. 'Yes, I think so.' He unscrewed the top of the carburettor, and checked its spring and the fluid.

His father had done all sorts of exotic modifications to gain a fraction more power from the engine.

Altering the strength of the damper spring or the viscosity of the oil could all eke out a fraction more horsepower or improve the acceleration of the car. He pulled at the accelerator cable and watched the action. He checked the oil level and the brake reservoir.

'Everything looks okay under the bonnet.' Kurt went round to the boot, opened it, and shone his torch inside. He looked under the spare tyre and pulled out a tool roll, wheel brace, and jack. Sophia looked at the jack and the tool roll. 'They were well prepared back then. These days all you get is the number of a breakdown company and an emergency tyre,' she said.

Kurt nodded. 'You said it.'

Sophia looked at the jack.'Could we use the jack to force the doors open?

'Worth a try,' Kurt said.

He reached into the car and flicked the lights on before taking the jack and wheel brace over to the back of the container. There was a small metal lip on the back door a few inches above the floor. Kurt slid the jack under it and pushed the wheel brace onto the bolt on one side of the jack.

'Here goes.' He slowly cranked the jack tighter. A miniscule glimmer of light spilled through a slit between the floor and the bottom of the door. The brace was becoming harder to twist and Kurt was having to exert more pressure with each turn.

'It's moving...' Sophia started to say, and then there was a screeching noise and the jack slammed shut like a crocodile's jaws.

'Damn it!' Kurt looked at the jack. 'We'd need a truck jack to crank our way out of here.'

'We have more gold in this truck than Midas and it's worthless to us,' Sophia said. She looked back to the tarpaulin-covered statue at the far end of the container.

'How much do you think it's worth?'

'Depends on the price of gold.'

'To the nearest million,' Sophia said with a smile.

He wiggled his fingers and Sophia could see his lips moving as he worked it out.'So, I'm going with dollars at sixteen ounces a pound, that's twenty-four thousand dollars a pound. And at two thousand pounds a ton...I'm not going to get into the whole short tons and long tons discussion here.'

'Thank God,' Sophia said.

Kurt went on. 'So that's two thousand times twenty-four thousand dollars...' Again, she could practically hear his brain calculating the figures. He finally looked up. 'Forty-eight million dollars a ton...'

'And how much does the sculpture weigh?

'The newspaper said it weighed five tons, but I'm not sure if that was the entire collection of statues or just one, like the "Bathing Ladies". Even if it was just five tons, that would make it worth around two hundred and forty million dollars.' 'I imagine that would grease a lot of palms at the terminal,' Sophia said.

Kurt looked around the container. 'We have to get out of this mausoleum before we're stacked up like so many metal coffins on a ship.' The container lurched as the truck moved forwards, winding its way through the terminal complex until it came to a halt. 'Okay, I'm guessing we're through security by now, but considering my knowledge of container terminals is what I remember from Iron Man 3, you're going to have to help me out here,' Sophia said.

'I have a rough idea. Once we're through security we go to a designated grid reference and an automatic gantry crane lifts the container off the truck and takes it to its slot,' Kurt said. The truck engine stopped and they heard the distant rumble of an approaching vehicle. Sophia headed for the Mini. 'C'mon, this is your chance to live your childhood dream,' Sophia said.

Kurt ran to the mini and jumped into the driver's seat. 'There's going to be one helluva' mess if this doesn't work.'

Sophia tightened her seat belt. 'Yes, and we don't have an airbag to save us.'

Kurt turned the ignition key and churned the starter motor. The engine coughed. Once. Twice. And fired.

Sophia looked at Kurt. 'We have to time this just right. As soon as you hear the crane hooking up with the container we hit the gas,' Sophia said.

'I'm good with that.' Kurt engaged reverse and slowly edged back until the bumper hit the statue under the tarpaulin.

The rumble of the approaching crane grew louder until the sound of it filled the container. Kurt gripped the steering wheel. In his mind he could hear the anthemic sound of *The Self Preservation Society* song from *The Italian Job* film, and found himself humming it. Sophia nudged him. 'Get ready,' Kurt smiled. And in a bad cockney accent said. 'I'm going to blow the bloody doors off.'

'Is this to do with your Mini film?' Sophia asked.

'Yes, sorry.' The container shook and there was a metallic thud from above as the gantry crane locked onto the top of the container. 'That's it!' Sophia said. Kurt put the Mini into first, released the handbrake, revved the engine until the head valves bounced and dropped the clutch. The front wheels left a trail of rubber and the Mini rocketed towards the container doors.

KABOOM!

CHAPTER FORTY-SIX

TEN MINUTES EARLIER

Hoog pulled up at the entrance to the container storage area. A bewildering array of containers stacked on top of each other towered above him. Gantry cranes were busy straddling containers, plucking their designated cargo from the pile before carrying them away to be loaded onto the waiting ships.

Robot-guided Terminal Tractors hummed past them on their way to unload and load smaller cargos, following a grid laid out within their digital cortex.

'How the hell are we going to find them in this maze?' Hoog said.

Ward looked up from his screen. 'I've got overhead visuals from the drone and the port authorities have given me access to the container storage plans.'

His screen filled with a stream of data and

schematics of the stacking plans throughout the terminal.

Katja stared at the digital rush hour. 'There's thousands of containers and we're running out of time.'

Ward nodded, 'We'll find them.'

He was as fond of Sophia as Katja and Hoog were. When he'd first joined the force, she'd set him straight on the difference between the rule book and protecting his own life. She'd spent many evenings teaching him basic martial art moves, and pressure points for close combat situations. He owed her.

'I have a plan.' Hoog and Katja looked at him.

'Make it quick, they could end up being buried in the middle of hundreds of tons of containers on the dock, or being loaded into a ship while we're talking.' Hoog said.

Ward looked down at the screen as hundreds of lines of freight details scrolled by. 'We have to assume the truck plates and the unique identifying number on the container were changed.'

'So how are you going to find it if we don't know what we're looking for?' Hoog asked.

Ward kept his eyes glued to the screen. 'By filtering. There are five container terminals and the average loading rate of the cranes is forty per hour, so I've discounted any container trucks that entered the port more than an hour ago. Then I've narrowed it down further by only adding containers with ventilation...' 'Is that because they've got Sophia and Kurt in the truck?' Katja asked.

Kurt shook his head. 'Nothing that altruistic I'm afraid. They're transporting a car so they wouldn't be allowed a container that couldn't vent any build-up of petrol fumes.'

'How many does that take it down to?' Katja asked.

'Just under a hundred, but when I filter out everything not going to St Petersburg we're down to forty containers.' Ward's fingers danced across the keys. 'Removing containers less than twelve metres in length gives us thirty potential candidates.'

Katja pulled her notebook out from her pocket. 'Can you filter by weight?' Katja said.

Ward turned to her. 'For sure.' Katja flicked through her notebook. 'Okay, the fully laden weight of the container comes out as 8531k, or 9.40 tons. That doesn't include petrol used or if the driver had a shit.'

Ward smiled, 'Okay, let's see.' His fingers tapped in the numbers and the stream of figures slowed. 'There's four of them within those parameters,' Ward said. He switched to the drone camera. A display ran beside the view indicating GPS coordinates. 'I'm feeding in the coordinates of the containers that have already been loaded, and if the truck is moving I can track it.'

The drone view twisted sickeningly as it spiralled down towards the stacked containers before straightening up and skimming across a sea of metal. It weaved around the gantry cranes that were busy depositing or removing individual containers. The drone hovered over a container sitting on the top of a vertiginous stack piled six high. Ward zoomed in on the identifying numbers on the side of the container. He punched up a CCTV picture of the back of the truck from the weighing machine printout in the Maldagem foundry, comparing the other marks and scratches with the container at the port.

'That's not it. One down, three to go.' The drone sped off, honing in on the next set of GPS coordinates.

'Damn!' 'What is it?' Hoog asked. 'Look,' Ward pointed at the screen. The drone showed a blank space between a row of stacked containers. 'Where is it?' Katja asked. Ward shook his head. 'It must be in transit, or being loaded. I have coordinates of all the gantry cranes in play at the moment, I'll do a sweep of them and see if any of them have our container.' The drone rose higher until its viewpoint encompassed the entire terminal. 'There's five terminals in all, and three cranes working in this one.' The drone swooped down, zeroing in on the first crane. Ward tapped some more keys and the picture of the container ran alongside the CCTV picture. A myriad of tracking points and grids flickered between them both until an icon blinked at the bottom of the screen: NO MATCH. 'What are you doing now?' Katja asked.

'I've linked some pattern recognition software to the drone's camera feed. It'll work through the crane coordinates until we find one with patterns matching our original container.' Hoog and Katja looked at the Tesla's display as the drone and the recognition software did their thing. Five minutes later, and the drone was headed back to locate the last two container coordinates. The drone hovered over a container sitting on the floor next to a single stack near the quayside. Ward compared the container.

'No match. There's only one left.'

The drone soared high above the quayside and hovered in the air, awaiting instructions. Ward tapped the tracker pad and the drone leant forwards and shot off on its mission. Within a minute it was hovering over an empty slot further down the quay.

'Where is it?' Hoog asked.

Ward tapped some keys searching for more information. 'There's a crane heading for these coordinates; if it's our man he's cutting it fine.' As they watched, a container lorry rumbled towards the empty slot and pulled up alongside the stack of containers. An icon winked in the corner of the screen: MATCH. Hoog pointed to the transfer running along the top of the truck's windscreen.

IF IT'S TOO LOUD THEN YOU'RE TOO OLD.

Ward pulled up the CCTV freeze frame of the truck leaving the foundry. The windscreen sticker matched.

'That's it,' Ward said. Hoog started the Tesla 'Okay, can you feed me the GPS coordinates?' Ward smiled. 'Already done.' The Tesla lunged forward, speeding down the quayside. And as they saw the truck, in the distance all hell broke loose.

CHAPTER FORTY-SEVEN

KABOOM! Hoog and Katja stared at the rear doors of the shipping container as the Mini exploded through them, slamming down onto the quayside and swerving sideways as the driver fought to bring it under control. Ward zoomed in to the Mini windscreen from the drone and focussed on the passenger.

'It's Sophia, and I'm guessing that's Kurt driving.' There was a burst of machine gun fire as the driver of the truck fired at the escaping car.

Hoog punched the talk button on his Coms unit. 'Detective Hoog, we need backup at quadrant 335. Armed men with automatic machine guns, proceed with extreme caution.'

The Mini veered right and accelerated down a steel

canyon of containers. Ward sent the drone shooting up high and immediately spotted two black SUVs in pursuit. A man leaned out of the side window of the SUV and let off a fusillade of shots at the fleeing Mini.

'We need to run interference until the DSU team arrives,' Hoog said.

Ward shook his hands, cracked his knuckles and grinned. 'And my mother said computer games were a waste of time.' His fingers flew across the tracker pad, and his screen filled with a graphic overlay of the terminal. The Mini was clearly visible, along with the two SUVs on its tail. Katja and Hoog watched the drone display on the Tesla dash screen. 'What are you doing?' Hoog asked.

Ward stared at his screen. 'We don't have control of where Kurt is going, but we do know the bad guys will be right behind him. The good news is that the Mini is far more manoeuvrable than the SUVs.'

Hoog nodded; from the drone's viewpoint he could see the SUVs gaining in a straight line but losing their advantage on the sharp turns around the stacked containers.

Katja looked at the drone's POV on the Tesla display. 'Why do crooks always drive black Range Rovers with black alloys. I mean, it screams drug dealer. Why don't they mix it up a bit, maybe go for a nice red colour.'

'Well I guess it wouldn't show any bloodstains.' Hoog said.

Katja looked to Ward. 'Do you have a plan?'

Ward nodded, fingers flying as coordinates streamed beneath his overview of the terminal. 'I do. It's going to be like digital Jenga. I've got control of the overhead gantry cranes and the ADVs. He looked up from his screen to clarify.

'Automatic driverless vehicles. I need to get Kurt onto a straight run.' The display switched to a graphic of the various potential routes through the maze of stacked containers. Ward tapped an icon on the screen and a crane moved into position, a container dangling from its jib. Ward lowered it down to seal off a left turn, forcing the mini and the pursuing SUVs to continue in a straight line between the stacked containers.

The rows of containers stretched for hundreds of metres before ending in a right turn. 'They're gaining on them,' Hoog said.'It's okay, I've got this,' Ward said. He took control of another overhead gantry crane, and swung a container towards a right-hand turn ahead of the Mini and the SUVs. He lowered the container towards the alleyway leading from the right-hand side.'If you block that off they'll be trapped,' Hoog said.

Ward kept his eyes on the screen. 'I'm not trapping them, just giving the bad guys a haircut.' The display switched back to a visual of the crane lowering the container down into the alleyway. 'One point five metres should do it,' Ward said.

The crane stopped lowering the container, and seconds later the Mini drifted around the corner and shot beneath it. The SUVs weren't so lucky. The leading SUV smashed into the gap beneath the container, shattering its windscreen, and buckling the side pillars. The SUV following concertinaed into it. Seconds later armed gunmen forced their way out of the wreckage. Ward tapped the crane icon and lowered the container to the ground, sealing the gunmen off. 'Shit,' Hoog pointed to a convoy of three more SUVs approaching from the other side of the terminal. 'Looks like we have some uninvited guests coming to the party,' he said.

Ward nodded, 'I see them...just got a bit of housekeeping to do here.' He tapped the gantry crane icon and sent it swooping down to pick up another container. 'Down you go.' The crane lowered its container down behind the wrecked SUVs, sealing off the gunmen's retreat. 'That should slow them down.'

'They've stopped,' Katja said, looking at the display showing the stationary Mini. 'Maybe they're out of fuel?' Hoog said. On the display the three approaching SUVs had split up, and were travelling down different routes, all of which led them towards the Mini.

Katja looked at the screen. 'I don't think they're out of fuel. I think Sophia has worked out she has some guardian angels, and the default position if you're lost or injured is to stay put until someone comes to get you.'

Hoog smiled. 'Clever girl. Now we only have to worry about the SUVs, and not where the Mini's headed.'

Ward swiped the tracker pad and a graphic of the terminal and the projected routes of the SUVs with ETA's beneath them filled the screen. The shortest ETA was just over a minute. His fingers flew over the keyboard, taking control of five separate gantry cranes. Within seconds, containers were swinging through the air, following their own digital coordinates, lowering their containers into a pre-ordained grid, sealing off the potential routes of the SUVs. One by one they reached the blocked routes.

'That should confuse the hell out of them,' Ward said.

Hoog pointed to the drone screen. 'We've got some foot soldiers headed their way.'

'Where the hell's the DSU?' Katja said.

'We need to get them out of there. Can you make a hole?' Hoog said.

Ward nodded. 'No problem.'

He took control of the gantry cranes and the ADV tractors, creating a pathway through the containers towards where the Mini was parked. Hoog sent the Tesla hurtling down the avenue of containers.

'Easy.' Ward said, struggling to keep hold of his laptop.

Hoog took his hands off the wheel. 'Don't blame me. I'm just a passenger. The Tesla has the coordinates and the timescale we have to meet.

Katja shook her head. 'Now I feel really safe.' She looked at the Tesla display. It showed an SUV travelling down between an alleyway of containers, headed for the Mini. A shadow passed over the SUV and the driver barely had time to flick a look up before a container pinned him from above. 'Oops,' Ward said. Hoog shot him a look. 'They'll be okay right?' Ward smiled.

'Of course, it was an empty container. They might feel a little cramped, but they'll be fine.'

Ward looked at the screen, focussing his attention on another SUV headed for the Mini. 'Time for a sandwich,' Ward said.

On the screen two ADV tractors began to move, while the SUV headed towards a T-junction at the end of a canyon of containers. The SUV entered the junction -- and never left. Two ADV tractors slammed into it from either side--a twenty ton steel vice. 'Uh Oh,' Ward said. 'What?' Hoog said.

'They've dumped the other SUV; we've got multiple foot soldiers headed towards the Mini.' Hoog looked at the screen and the Tesla ETA reading. 'We'll get there before them. I'm going to manual.' Ward tapped something on the screen. 'What are you doing now?' Katja asked. 'Booking an Uber,' Ward said.

Hoog threw the Tesla round a corner, speeding across junctions, weaving past parked containers and ADVs, and suddenly the stationary Mini was in front of them. The Tesla slid to a halt. Katja jumped out and ran towards the car. Sophia climbed out and hugged her. 'Thank God you're safe.'

'Don't I get a hug?' Kurt said with a smile from the driver's seat.

Katja smiled back. 'Not yet, after all this was you're idea.'

'Guilty as charged,' Kurt said.

'Get into the Tesla,' Katja said. Sophia and Kurt ran to the Tesla, ducking under its falcon wing doors as they arched open. A burst of fire from overhead rattled off the protective cover of the falcon wings as Kurt slid into the back seat next to Ward, and Sophia dived through the open passenger door, slamming it shut as a bullet ricocheted off one of the containers beside them.

Hoog climbed out of the driver's seat and joined Katja crouched behind the Tesla. He whipped out his Glock and fired a quick volley of shots towards their attackers. A gunman on a distant container stumbled backwards clutching at his shoulder before tumbling to the ground. Hoog slipped a wireless ear-pod into one ear and an earpiece from his coms unit into the other. He tapped the screen on his mobile.

Katja flicked him a look. 'Dua Lipa?' she asked.

'Seems appropriate,' Hoog replied, pulling out a pair of Glock 9mm magazines taped together from his black holdall, and sliding them into the pistol. The Tesla side window hummed down.

Ward looked out at the elongated magazine. 'That's a monster,' he said.

Hoog nodded. '64 round reversible magazine. It's a bit of a handful, but once I'm in position, I'll be on my own.'

'Not exactly,' Ward said. 'What's your plan?'

'I need you to get me above those bad guys.'

Ward looked down at the drone view of the terminal. 'Okay, fifty metres to your left there's a pile of wooden pallets that gives you access onto a container. You'll be shielded on both sides, and I can get you above the action. I'll feed target references and a drone POV to your mobile. I just need to connect the twist locks to the container and we're all set.'

'Sounds good,' Hoog said. He ducked as more shots ricocheted off the Tesla's bodywork. Ward's fingers flew across the tracker pad and a crane swung towards them, its jaws spooling down.

'Turn your laser sight on,' Ward said. Hoog activated

the DLP laser sight on the Glock. A thin beam of red light winked out from beneath the barrel.

Hoog nodded. 'Done.'

Ward tapped some icons on the screen. 'I'm using the GPS on your mobile and synching it with the drone coordinates. Check your phone.' Hoog pulled out his mobile and saw the drone POV. 'Now bring your gun up.'

Hoog levelled the Glock. An image of the gun barrel appeared on his mobile, along with an infrared track showing the beam from his laser sight.

'You'll be able to target the bad guys without exposing yourself.' Hoog gave him a look.

'You know what I mean,' Ward said with a smile. 'Like a first-person shoot-em-up,' Hoog said. 'Exactly. The container will shield you from below and the only thing higher than you will be the drone. Okay, the container's in place,' Ward said.

Hoog turned to Katja, 'Stay in the Tesla till it's safe. Okay?'

Katja nodded. 'You know where I am if you need backup,' she said, climbing into the passenger seat.'For sure,' Hoog said.

He broke cover from behind the Tesla, sending a withering burst of fire towards the nearest gunmen. Seconds later Hoog was scrambling up the wooden pallets onto the top of the container, flattening himself on the cold metal as Ward sent it soaring into the sky. Hoog looked at his mobile and saw the first-person overlay synched with his laser and the drone's overhead view. He pointed his gun over the edge of the container and targeted the gunman firing towards the Tesla.

'Game over,' he said, snapping off a couple of shots. The gunman pirouetted off the top of the container and tumbled out of sight. Hoog swung the Glock around, searching for fresh targets.

The image of two gunmen crouched on a nearby container filled the mobile screen. Hoog loosed off two more shots, and the gunmen crumpled. He swung the Glock to the left searching for more targets. Which is when the mobile battery died.

'Shit!' Hoog shuffled back from the edge of the container and keyed his comms unit. 'Hi Ward, gotta' bit of a problem. My mobile's died. Can you give me the heads-up on some targets?

Ward's voice crackled out of the comms unit. 'You got it. The way you're facing is one o'clock, you got a hotspot at twelve o'clock.'

'Copy that.' Hoog nodded his head to the beat of the Dua Lipa track in his ear, psyching himself up for his assault. He peered over the edge of the container, angling himself towards twelve o' clock below. He saw two black-clad figures pointing their guns at him from the container below. He fired off two rounds and they hit the deck.

Ward's voice crackled from the comms unit.'Five o' clock and eight o' clock.' Hoog ducked as a torrent of bullets rattled against the side of the container. He looked over and returned fire towards the two coordinates, taking down two more gunmen.

'Gotcha!' Hoog said.

Ward's voice crackled in his earpiece. 'Time for you to leave Hoog. Too many bad guys heading our way. I'm bringing you back in.'

Ward dragged his eyes off the laptop screen and spoke to Kurt. 'Any idea why your arrival has triggered all-out Armageddon?' 'Long story short, we appear to have been travelling biscuit class with a quarter of a billion euros worth of gold,' Kurt said.

'I can't wait for the long version of that. Just got to tidy up a few things here first,' Ward said, his fingers flying across the tracker pad.

'Okay. Hoog's back down. Standby for incoming. Kurt, get ready to move. You have a small window of opportunity before the next wave of bad guys appear over the horizon.'

Katja looked through the windscreen of the Tesla as

a shadow slid over them, and an open-ended container settled on the ground with a dull thump.

Kurt jumped out of the Tesla and ran to the Mini. Within seconds he'd driven it into the container. Sophia clambered into the back seat of the Tesla next to Ward, as Hoog appeared and jumped behind the wheel.'Time to leave the party,' he said, closing the falcon wing doors as another burst of gunfire clattered against the bodywork. Hoog stamped on the accelerator and shot towards the open container, braking hard behind the Mini inside. Within seconds the container was airborne.

'So, is this what you meant by an Uber?' Katja shouted over the staccato rattle of bullets from the gunmen below as they skimmed over the containers beneath them. 'I like to be prepared for all eventualities,' Ward said. 'Got anything else up your sleeve?' Katja asked.

'I have a little something that might help the clean-up squad,' he said. Katja looked at the drone's eye view on the Tesla display. A gantry crane swung a cylindrical chemical truck over the sea of containers below. Five or six gunmen were headed towards where the Mini used to be, while a DSU team shadowed them through a parallel alleyway of containers. 'I've given the DSU squad leader the drone feed so he knows where the bad guys are,' Ward said. The gunmen looked up as the cylindrical truck swung over them. Ward tapped some keys. 'Here we go.' A torrent of brown sludge rained down on the gunmen, sending them choking to their knees. 'What is that?' Katja asked. 'Same shit, different day,' Ward said with a grin. 'Agricultural slurry, liquid silage.'

Katja looked at the gasping men. 'Manure.' 'Right first time. I don't think the K-9 unit will have too much trouble sniffing them out. Do you?'

CHAPTER FORTY-EIGHT

The Tesla reversed out of the container, followed by the Mini. They came to a halt and everyone climbed out of the cars and stretched their legs.

'What happened to the statue?' Sophia asked. 'It's being kept somewhere safe until the powers that be decide what to do with it,' Hoog said.

Sophia gave a derisory snort. 'That's rich. When it was five tons of bronze they just left it on a piece of wasteland, now that it's worth a quarter of a billion euros they keep it in a safe place.'

Hoog smiled. 'You should get into politics with your easy-going charm and devil may care attitude.'

Sophia looked at him. 'For sure. I feel a waffle coming on, and a heap of paperwork. But first of all, I'd like to thank Ward and Kurt for their outstanding nerdy skills, without which I doubt if any of us would still be here.' They all muttered thanks.

Hoog clapped Ward on the shoulder. 'No doubt about that. I say we head back to the station and get some coffee down our necks. It's going to be a long night.'

CHAPTER FORTY-NINE

Chief Nils Janssen sat behind his desk, with his fingers steepled and a fresh cup of coffee and biscuits in front of him. His assistant was just leaving. She flashed a look at Hoog, who sat next to Katja, Sophia and Ward.

'Would you like anything else?' she asked. 'I think we're all waffled up thank you.' Hoog said. Nils took another sip of coffee. They'd been working through the night and he'd lost count of how many cups of coffee he'd consumed.

Between the mayor and the head of port authorities his ear had been clamped to one kind of phone for most of the night. The body count had been high, the reaction to the destruction wrought at the Antwerp terminal even higher.

The fact that none of his officers or civilians had been amongst the casualties would help mitigate the fallout in the upcoming press coverage.

His PA had delivered a selection of the morning papers and he glanced at a headline that screamed: *'Police in nightmare game of terminal Jenga.'* And that was one of the less lurid headlines that begged for his attention. The previous day's events were going to keep the press and the insurance companies busy for a long, long time. His favourite front page was a picture of the Mini Cooper 'S' in mid-air, snatched from CCTV footage with the headline:

"The Italian Job comes to Antwerp"

At least he was old enough to get the reference. He put his coffee cup down and offered the plate of biscuits around the table. Everyone waved them away except Ward, who picked up a ginger biscuit.

'My favourite.' Nils put the plate down. 'Okay, I would have asked Kurt to join us as he was an essential part of the operation, and undoubtedly responsible for saving lives. But I think we might have some bureaucratic issues. So, if it's alright with everyone, I'll let you bring him up to speed in the fullness of time and at your own discretion.' He looked around and acknowledged the unanimous nods of agreement.

'I imagine he'll be putting his own spin on events in due course, and as no one has come forward to claim ownership of the Mini, I think he'll be more than happy to get his hands on that as well,' Hoog said.

'I'm sure,' Nils agreed. He paused. 'The attack on the police by the criminal gang at the port is a matter for the Antwerp authorities to deal with, and their interrogation of those in custody is ongoing. There is of course an overlap with that incident and the discovery of the statue stolen from t'Zand Square in the container. From our initial investigation we have established some details of the operation and its scope. A lot of this information which was initially supposition has been proven to be factual, and most of it has been uncovered in no small part by our good friend Kurt, who I have to say, up till now I had completely misjudged.'

'I think you used the expression conspiracy nut,' Hoog prompted.'

'Indeed,' Nils said. 'But as we now know, his theories turned out to have a basis in fact.'

'That's for sure,' Hoog agreed.

Nils took a sip of coffee before continuing, 'Okay, so Antwerp will deal with the fallout from the port, and they've released the statue into our custody. But we do have an interesting situation concerning its ownership and valuation.'

'I take it they're unaware of its true value?' Hoog said.

Nils nodded. 'At present yes. I'm keeping that within this group, and Kurt, obviously.'

'Is there a chance we may have to involve Europol or Interpol in the investigation Chief?' Katja asked. 'Considering we have a statue worth over a quarter of billion euros that's a very big possibility,' Nils said.

'If this is only one part of the puzzle we could be looking at an operation worth billions,' Katja said.

Nils nodded. 'I contacted a friend of mine in the art and forgeries division in Antwerp and asked him to check the most recent statue that was stolen and then recovered.' 'The Sleeping Child?' Katja asked.

'Yes. He took a scraping from a part of the statue not normally visible.'

'Gold?' Hoog asked.

The Chief nodded, 'Yes, beneath a patina of potash and ferric nitrate. On paper it's worth millions.'

Ward looked over at Hoog. 'If Kurt's research is accurate, and I have no reason to believe otherwise, we are talking upwards of a hundred or more statues that have been substituted over the course of the operation.'

Nils nodded. 'As you know, Erika finally remembered the name of the Russian organisation her friend told her about. It was called *Plintus...Plinth* in English. I think the name confirms what we already know about their agenda, though we have no idea how many people are involved,' Nils said.

Katja leaned forwards and took a biscuit, chewing slowly as she thought things through. 'So we're saying the Russians have been using *Plinth* to track down stashes of stolen gold that went missing after the Romanovs were executed. Utilising a global network to steal statues, using them as moulds to make a solid gold copy.'

'Yes,' Nils said. 'And Kurt was the only person to detect a pattern in what was going on,' Hoog said.

'A pattern that changed when the t'Zand Square statue was stolen,' Katja said. 'Yes,' Hoog said. 'Someone got greedy and planned to keep the gold for themselves.'

'So why was there such a delay in returning the t'Zand Square statue? After all, they only had to replace the original statue rather than a gold copy and then make off with the Romanov gold and no one would have been any the wiser,' Katja said.

Ward dunked a ginger biscuit into his coffee and took a bite before speaking. 'I think they had a problem retrieving the gold from the U-boat; after all it was a highly complex operation. Getting the dredger in place in the middle of a major shipping lane, finding a diver willing to risk getting into the U-boat, and locating a foundry they could use without arousing suspicion.'

'Maybe they jumped the gun, destroyed the original

statue and then realised getting the gold out of the U-boat wasn't going to be that easy.' Hoog said.

Katja nodded. 'Whatever its failings it's still a work of genius. By storing the gold off the books they wouldn't flood the gold market and crash the financial system. And if they run short of gold and need to bolster their gold reserves they just steal a statue and voila, they have a cash injection of millions of roubles. It's like a Freeport without any of the paperwork.'

Hoog looked at Nils. 'So, if we were to blow this conspiracy wide open we'd flood the gold market, destroy the Russian financial system, and kick a hornet's nest when it comes to establishing who actually owns the gold, both historically and politically.'

'Jesus. What the hell are you going to do?' Katja said.

Nils steepled his hands together. 'Well I'm open to suggestions, let's put it that way. The Antwerp port authorities intercepted a container truck trying to leave the terminal after the shootout, and found the rest of the duplicate 't Zand statues inside.'

'So we're looking at a lot more than five tons if we count the entire collection,' Katja said.'You're looking at almost half a billion euros,' Ward said.

Hoog smiled. 'And they say you can never have too much money.'

'Except in this case,' Nils said, rubbing his face with his hands. The phone on his desk jangled. He picked the phone up and spoke. 'Chief Janssen.' He listened. His face sagged. 'I can be there in just over an hour. Okay.' He put the phone down.

'That was the Russian ambassador calling from their embassy in Brussels. He wants to see me for an informal chat.' 'See," Hoog said, 'Things can always get worse.'

They left the Chief grumbling behind his desk and walked down Woolestraat, over the Dijver canal and swung a right beside the canal before taking a left down the Groeninge towards the Museum. Hanna had texted Katja and suggested a meet. She'd been trying to find if there was any connection between the stolen Basilica relic and Marsha and Brandt Van Zwart's appearance in Venice. Whatever it was she'd found, Hanna was eager to share. Though he'd been looking forward to putting his feet up, rather than disappearing down some historical rabbit hole, Hoog decided it might be a good idea to beat a retreat before Janssen returned from his meet with the Russian Ambassador. Whatever the Ambassador had to say, he felt sure that it wouldn't improve the Chief's demeanour. Politics and policing were never a happy mix.

CHAPTER FIFTY

Hanna and Erika were waiting in the storeroom beneath the museum when they arrived, and Hoog was glad to see a plate heaped with Hanna's home-made biscuits along with some steaming mugs of fresh coffee. He swooped on the biscuits and bit into one with satisfaction.

'Mmm, is that ginger?' he asked between mouthfuls.

'With Belgian white chocolate and some raisins thrown in for good measure,' Hanna replied, smiling.

'So, what have you found?' Hoog asked. Erika nodded to Hanna.

'Hanna's been going through the case notes of the Louisiana investigation, and the theft of the holy relic from the basilica.'

'You mean Ward of course, as Hanna wouldn't have access to police files,' Katja said with a wink.

'Of course, my mistake,' Erika said.

'I'll agree to anything for another biscuit,' Ward said.

'I think we can waive the legal niceties for the moment, and assume Hanna is a consultant in our investigation,' Hoog said.

'Go on Hanna,' Erika said. Hanna pointed to a corkboard covered in printouts of various artefacts linking Jesus Christ and the mythology surrounding the holy blood. 'I did a search for similar reliquaries involving Christ's blood, to see if there was any link to Venice.'

'Do you think Marsha's planning more thefts? And if so, why?' Katja asked.

Hanna pointed to the corkboard. 'I'll get back to the "why" in a minute. But first you'll need some background,' she tapped the pictures on the corkboard before speaking.

'The Dominican Rosary promoted devotion to the five wounds of Christ. One through each hand or wrist, one through each foot and one to the chest. So, let's look at the usual suspects in the search for Christ's blood. The Turin Shroud, widely believed to be an elaborate fake by the artist involved,' she tapped another picture.

'The spear supposedly used by centurion Gaius Cassius Longinus to stab Christ on the cross.'

'Didn't Hitler have a thing for that?' Hoog asked.

Erika nodded. 'The so called "Spear of Destiny," he used it to justify his campaign for world domination and the creation of an Aryan master race. Go on Hanna.'

'We also have the Sudarium of Oviado, the bloody cloth wrapped around Jesus's head after his death and kept in the cathedral of San Salvador in Spain. Its authenticity is as widely disputed as the Turin Shroud. Then there's the crucifixion nails. The iron crown of Lombardy, kept in a cathedral outside of Milan, was supposedly made from one of the nails.' Hanna paused, before going on.

'I won't include the Holy Grail, I think Indiana Jones and Dan Brown have already covered that particular myth, so next up would be the "Crown of Thorns," supposedly housed at the Notre Dame cathedral in Paris, again, no real proof of its authenticity. And the final contender is the weirdest. She tapped a picture of a small alabaster container on the board.

'The Holy Prepuce...'

'The what?' Hoog asked.

Hanna smiled. 'The holy foreskin. Jewish tradition would have called for Christ to have been circumcised, and according to New Testament apocryphal writing on the infancy of Christ, the foreskin was saved in an alabaster box.'

'For real?' Katja wrinkled her nose, ' apparently, in

the Middle Ages, foreskin "relics" were commonplace, with as many as 18 circulating in Europe simultaneously. In 1900 the Catholic Church decreed that anyone even talking about The Holy Prepuce would be excommunicated. As far as anyone knows, there are no more holy foreskins in existence.' Hanna waited for a reaction.

Katja shook her head. 'I'm still trying to get the image of Christ's foreskin out of my mind.'

'It certainly has a high yuk factor,' Hanna said.

'So now we've endured that, what's their connection to the basilica theft,' Katja said.

'I promised I would get back to you with the 'why',' Hanna said. 'In 1490 a secret order was established in Venice called Christos Immortalis Sanguis, literally translated as the immortal blood of Christ.'

'And what were they up to back then?' Hoog asked, reaching for another biscuit.

'Well, the clue's in the name really. They believed that they could use the blood of Christ to gain immortality,' Hanna said. 'Like Voodoo queen Marsha's quest for immortality for her late lover Roman Blackburn, and his most recent incarnation, Brandt Van Zwart,' Katja said.

Hoog nodded. 'He does bear an uncanny resemblance to the late Roman Blackburn.'

'Yes, and if we find them in Venice maybe we can solve that particular mystery,' Katja said. 'From the evidence found in Spirit's Swamp, and the notes Roxie made at the scene, it seems Marsha and Blackburn were attempting to regrow human cells using some kind of crude gene editing and stem cell blood from umbilical cords...though from the pictures of dead foetus's that the detectives found beneath the old orphanage it didn't look like their experiments were very successful,' Hanna said.

'How does this connect with Venice, religious reliquaries and a secret order in the 15th century?' Hoog asked.

'I had to do a bit of research into gene editing to make sense of it, but Roxie's notes helped. You need to amass a certain amount of DNA information to create enough cells to clone a genetic match,' Hanna said.

Hoog rubbed his eyes. 'Like Dolly the sheep back in the 90's.'

'Yes, and we've come a long way since then,' Hanna said.

'So if they collected enough of Christ's DNA from religious reliquaries they could edit the samples together into a complete strand of DNA? Katja asked. Hanna looked at her.

'In theory that would give you enough DNA to create a clone of Jesus, and along with that, immortality.' Ward had been listening intently. It wasn't his area of expertise and he was struggling to keep up. Finally, he spoke.

'But from what you said earlier, it seems like all of these reliquaries are mythical objects for the faithful and the tourists to visit...there's no real proof that any of them contain Christ's blood in reality.'

Hoog nodded. 'I agree, it's all a bit Dan Brown to me,' he said.

'That maybe,' Hanna said. 'But that doesn't stop Marsha and Brandt Van Zwart believing they can achieve their aims. And depending on Marsha's shamanistic abilities, she may actually be able to locate which, if any, of these objects contain traces of Christ's DNA.'

'But none of the reliquaries you talked about are in Venice,' Hoog said.

Hanna said, 'As far as we know, but I don't think you stumbled onto a Facebook page with Marsha and her friend on a gondola by chance. I think Marsha wanted you to go to Venice.'

'You think it's another ploy to draw us in, like they set up Chandler, Duke and Roxie to get revenge on them for what happened in Louisiana?' Hoog said.

'If that's the case they could be walking into a trap, Katja said.

Hoog shook his head. 'No way are they going to walk into a trap, not after last time. They'll be on the lookout for anything like that. Though it can't do any harm to give them a heads up.'

'I agree,' Hanna said, reaching for some printouts. 'The order had a specific kind of member. Scientists, physicians, visionaries and devout believers in reincarnation, all of whom were risking their lives by even thinking such things back then. Formed in 1490, the order soon had one member whose visionary work and beliefs were way ahead of his time. In fact, it wasn't until hundreds of years after his death that some of his ideas were finally made a reality. He was an accomplished painter, sculptor, inventor and scientist.'

'Leonardo Da Vinci?' Hoog said.

Hanna smiled. 'Yes. He fled from Milan to Venice in 1500 when Lodovico Sforza, the then Duke of Milan, was overthrown by King Louis XII.'

'And why's that significant?' Hoog asked.

'Well, according to legend, the order's headquarters were based in Venice, somewhere so secret that it was never found. There are references to it being built to a design by Leonardo Da Vinci, and that it was invisible. What that means I don't know,' Hanna said.

'So what else do we know about Leonardo Da Vinci?' Ward asked.

'He did his first drawing in 1473 at the age of 21. It was a landscape of the Arno Valley where he was living. He was highly inquisitive, always wanting to find out about everything. His inquisitiveness even extended to the caves in the Apennine Mountains. They're a large hypogenic cave system, tens of kilometres long, with maze patterns, large rooms, cupola roofs, blindpits and anastomotic zones.'

Hoog held up his hand. 'I was on the floor after hypogenic, and anastomotic finished me off.'

Hanna smiled. 'Sorry. Hypogenic caves are formed by water rising from below ground and anastomotic zones are one of the maze cave patterns.'

'That's all clear now.' Hoog said.

Hanna went on. 'So, he wanders into this cave, who knows how long he's in there...and from that point on he becomes a polymath: painter, sculptor, architect, musician, scientist, mathematician, engineer, inventor, anatomist, geologist, cartographer, botanist and writer. He starts sketching all kinds of amazing inventions which won't become a reality for hundreds of years: helicopters, armoured fighting machines, the parachute, concentrated solar power, a calculator, a rudimentary theory of plate tectonics...not to mention submarines and diving suits.' Hanna paused. 'That is a bit weird.' Katja said. Hoog nodded, 'I wonder what he would have thought about Bill Gates buying one of his sketch books for over 30 million dollars.' Hanna smiled. 'I can't imagine. But Bill Gates sees himself as a kindred spirit to Leo. Even though he's not a creative artist he is a kind of visionary,' Hanna paused, before going on.

Back in 1999 he envisaged people carrying around a small device which would enable them to constantly keep in touch and carry out electronic business wherever they were.'

'The smartphone,' Ward said.

'Yes. And here's something Leonardo wrote in his diaries...' Hanna said. 'Didn't he write everything backwards so you could only read it in a mirror?' Katja asked.

Hanna nodded. 'Yes, he was left handed so it was easier for him to mirror his writing, and he also wrote in a special kind of shorthand that he invented himself.'

'Not that he was paranoid or anything,' Ward said. 'Exactly, luckily someone else did the translation.' Hanna picked up a printout and started reading. 'This is what he said about his *Machine for many people to stay underwater;* he kept the exact details of the machine secret because of...' Hanna looked at the paper. 'The evil nature of men who would use them as a means of destruction, sinking ships together with the men in them.'

'His sentiments predate the U-boat attacks by over six hundred years.' Erika said.

'I think we're all agreed Leonardo was a genius, but how does that help us?' Hoog asked. Hanna looked to Erika like a student looking to her professor before speaking. 'Leonardo was famous for many things, one of which was his amazing anatomical drawings; he was fascinated by how the human body worked and carried out over 400 dissections, so the belief in immortality through the use of Christ's blood would have made him a natural candidate to join the order.' Katja said, 'Okay, so we're talking about a genius who invented early versions of the helicopter, submarines and diving suits as well as the camera obscura...' Ward was busy tapping on his iPad. He held up a finger. 'The concept of the camera obscura and the pinhole camera was actually invented in the 6th century by Anthemius of Tralles.'

'Thank you, Detective Wikipedia. Nobody likes a smart arse,' Katja said. 'I guess Leo didn't have many friends then,' Ward said, smiling. 'Ha Ha,' Hanna said. 'Anyway, the last text we got from your colleague Roxie in Venice ended with her saying they were following in the footsteps of Leonardo da Vinci.' 'And that's why you're so interested in Leo,' Hoog said.

Hanna nodded. 'Yes, I emailed and texted her to ask what she meant but I haven't heard back yet. I just thought I'd do some research while I was waiting.''Could they have found out about the order?' Erika asked.

Hanna shrugged. 'I don't know, they may be on the trail of the order's headquarters,' Hanna said.

Katja looked at the corkboard and the printouts on the wall. She walked over to a printout of the iconic Vitruvian Man. 'Is it possible that the order had begun to collect religious reliquaries supposedly containing enough of Christ's blood to carry out their experiments into immortality,' she said.

'Maybe, but that was centuries before anybody had the slightest idea about blood transfusions or knew anything about genetic manipulation,' Hanna replied.

Erika nodded. 'Yes, which is why for centuries Marsha failed in her attempts to make her partners immortal, and had to resort to more socially unacceptable methods to continue the bloodline.'

'You mean incest?' Katja said.

She flashed back to her conversations with Aart de Vries in the Sint Janshospitaal museum. Vries had brought her up to speed on the history of witchcraft in Bruges, and *IGNIS*, the witches' super coven.

He'd explained about the mythology of self-immolation, the terrifying process that allowed Marja Nalangu to possess Marsha Brochell, the great granddaughter of Leatrice Brochell, the voodoo queen of New Orleans. Erika looked at her, 'Yes. Marsha might already know where the order's headquarters are, and that's why she's in Venice. The reliquary from the Basilica could be the last sample of DNA she needs for her plan to succeed.'

'I'm no expert, but surely any DNA on the relics would have degraded after hundreds of years?' Hoog said.

'No,' Katja said. 'It was one of the things I learnt

from Roxie. The half-life of DNA is approximately 521 years."So, the DNA could still be viable?' Hoog asked.'521 years is its half-life, the point at which half of the bonds in a DNA molecule are broken down. So, under ideal conditions DNA molecules would last about 6.8 million years,' Katja said. 'Shit, that is a long time,' Hoog said.

Katja laughed. 'That's an understatement. Roxie told me about the case of the Boston Strangler. They recovered fifty year old DNA from a blanket found at the crime scene and exhumed the body of the suspect, Albert De Salvo, to confirm the match.'

Hoog nodded. 'So, if there's any truth to this hidden headquarters story it could be where Marsha's headed. Failing that we have to assume they know of another source of DNA in Venice.'

'I guess we'll have to wait until Roxie gets back to us,' Katja said.

CHAPTER FIFTY-ONE

Nils sat in the imposing opulence of the ambassador's office in the Brussels embassy building. The walls were adorned with various stiffly posed pictures of dead and gone Russian heroes and royalty.

Nils looked across the room at a large portrait of Putin occupying pride of place behind the ambassador's seat. He'd had the distinct impression that the eyes had followed him around the room earlier, when the ambassador had talked him through the history of the various paintings on display.

A large black and white picture of the Romanov dynasty, taken in the same year they were executed, dominated one wall, as if to say: 'You can never have too much money.' Yuri leaned forward and steepled his hands. Nils quickly unsteepled his. He wasn't getting into some weird psychological mirroring contest.

'Thank you for coming so quickly. I imagine you have your hands full dealing with the fallout from yesterday's events.'

Nils smiled. He wasn't going to let an incident of that size be belittled by low-value adjectives. 'I don't think the word *'event'* fully encompasses the scale of what happened yesterday.'

Nils knew Yuri's English was impeccable, and his choice of words was carefully calculated to play down the situation.

Yuri nodded. His eyes gleamed as he fixed them on Nils. 'Excuse me, a poor choice of words. Maybe the expression clusterfuck would be more accurate?'

'Getting there,' Nils said.

'Okay. Let us cut to the chase. For many years we have had an imbalance of our gold reserves. And I am sure you are aware of our chequered past concerning the Romanov fortune.'

'I've heard a great many stories and conspiracy theories concerning the Romanov gold and where it ended up,' Nils said.

'Indeed, many books have been written and many more theories have been expounded over the years. Anyway, to the point. As I said, the parlous...? He paused. 'Parlous? This is correct?' Yuri asked.

Nils knew that Yuri had no confusion at all about the meaning of the word. 'You're trying to tell me you have fuck all gold reserves left.'

Yuri smiled. 'Fuck all, precisely. Well, bearing that in mind, it was agreed we should set up a unit to try and recover our missing gold and augment our shrinking reserves. The organisation was tasked with tracking down and recovering the gold, and to homogenise...again please excuse my English.'

'You melted it down,' Nils said.

'Yes. But if we located all of the Romanov gold and declared its existence it would create massive problems both politically and financially. Flooding the market with billions of roubles worth of gold would be catastrophic.'

'So, you decided it would be better for all of this recovered gold to disappear, to be kept off the books.'

'Yes. A state-backed agency was set up.'

'Plinth?' Nils said.

'Yes. It was called that for reasons that will have become obvious to you by now.'

'So, your state funded investigators to track down the Romanov gold and ferret it out of its many lairs around the world... and from beneath its oceans.'

'Yes. In retrospect we could have handled that particular recovery a little more discreetly,' Yuri said.

'Looting a sunken war grave in the middle of a busy shipping lane at night wasn't a great idea.'

'Smartphones are the curse of the twenty-first century,' Yuri said.

'But that wasn't your main problem though, was it?' Nils asked.

Yuri steepled his fingers, realised it wasn't going to work and un-steepled them before continuing. 'One should never underestimate the power of human greed.'

'Or the tenacity of the Belgian police.'

'Exactly. But as you yourself know, a lot of small things can combine to produce...what did you call it? A clusterfuck,' Yuri said.

'Yes. A petty thief couldn't resist the opportunity to steal some of the gold he helped recover and multiply his gains by forging it.'

'Yes, only the people he was working for weren't part of your state-backed organisation,' Nils said.

'No. They were a criminal gang running their own operation,' Yuri said, laying a copy of a charge sheet onto the table. The giant with the thick neck from the foundrey glowered at the camera.

'Olaf Grummel. An ex-FSB agent gone rogue He organised the theft of the original 't Zand statues from storage, and created a copy using stolen Romanov gold. Only instead of returning the statue they planned to ship it out of the country. We have him in custody and he'll be extradited to Moscow for questioning.'

'Yes. They could have planned to replace the genuine

statue to cover up their actions, but for now we have no idea where it is,' Yuri said.

'And this would only have come to light when you needed to top up your gold reserves and discovered the statue was bronze,' Nils said.

'Yes,' Yuri said.

'But it all fell apart when our conspiracy nut stuck his nose into your business.'

'Yes. Normally no one would have believed his suspicions, but with a forged Romanov gold ingot in the mix and your police detectives' tenacity, it began to unravel.'

'So, as it stands, your global Freeport operation, and *Plinth,* are under serious threat.'

Yuri nodded. 'Yes. If the operation your detectives have uncovered gets into the public domain it would be catastrophic.'

Nils didn't have to think too hard to imagine the reaction from the various governments, the legal claims on the Romanov gold, the press fallout and the never-ending paperwork that would strangle his department for years to come.

'I know what you're thinking,' Yuri said. Nils looked up at the picture of Putin. Again, he felt as if he was being watched. In fact, he was almost certain that their entire conversation was being filmed and uploaded to the digital cloud hanging over the Kremlin. He found it hard to believe Yuri knew what he was thinking, as he barely knew himself. 'So, tell me,' Nils said.

'You're thinking, do I really need all of this on my desk right now? The bureaucracy, the political...' he paused... 'shenanigans, and the years of paperwork.'

'That's a pretty accurate guess,' Nils said.

Yuri smiled. 'So, why go down that route, when the whole event could just be reported as the smashing of an international smuggling ring through exceptional police work.'

Nils thought about this. If there was one thing he hated about his job it was politics. And if there was a way out of the yawning chasm of politics and bureaucracy facing him he was prepared to hear Yuri's plan. 'Okay, so why don't you tell me how you think this is going to work.'

CHAPTER FIFTY-TWO

'A finder's fee?' Hoog said.

Nils nodded. 'He called it that, but officially it would be split into a multitude of smaller charitable donations across the police force.'

'Does this feel like a bribe to anyone?' Katja said.

'I think this is the point where someone says the phrase "Big picture,"' Sophia said, making air quotes.

'I agree. Turning them down flat would make me a little nervous when I remember how scary the Russians can be,' Katja said.

Nils nodded. 'Yuri assured me that whatever our collective decision concerning *Plinth* might be, our safety would be his paramount responsibility.'

Katja looked at Nils. 'That's fair enough Chief, but

what happens if he gets disappeared, who's going to be looking out for us then?'

Hoog said, 'As far as the Russians are concerned they've taken a legitimate action to protect their government and the financial stability of its people by stashing caches of recovered gold around the world. We're dealing with global theft, with the stolen statues supposedly being returned after a while, and the general public being none the wiser. If it hadn't been for Bakker wanting to feather his own nest, and Kurt's investigations, the statues would be sitting around the world until the Russian state needed to bolster its gold reserves. And at that point the Russians would have the statue stolen again.'

'So where are all the original statues? Ward asked.

'I didn't ask,' Nils said, 'I'm guessing they must store them somewhere.' 'What sort of finder's fee are we talking about?' Sophia asked.

Nils steepled his fingers. 'Ten per cent of the statue's value.'

Hoog did some rough calculations in his head. 'That's over ten million euros!'

'Does this mean we'll be getting a new coffee machine?' Sophia said.

'With that amount of money, you could probably buy your own coffee shop,' Katja said.

'Okay, whatever we decide, this has to be unanimous.

We'll take credit for smashing an international smuggling ring, and get our statue back, albeit worth slightly more than the original, dodge a ton of extra paperwork, and help the Russians avoid political and financial suicide,' Nils said, looking around for an opinion.

'So how much does the police force actually get out of the finder's fee?' Hoog asked.

'It's about nine and a half million euros to various pension funds, infrastructure improvements, free healthcare for disabled officers and a load of other benefits.'

'Where did the other half a million go? Ward asked.

'Yuri thought that a finder's fee of one hundred thousand euros to each of the officers involved and to Kurt would be appropriate,' Nils said. There was a hushed silence in the office.'Paid out in a controlled drawdown to avoid any ugly tax problems,' Nils paused. Vote?'

A slow Mexican wave spread around the assembled officers. It was unanimous.

'Okay. I'll let Yuri know and we can tie up any loose ends.' There was a knock at the door and Ward burst in, his face flushed with excitement.

'You need to see something.'

CHAPTER FIFTY-THREE

National Marine Park, Quintana Roo, Mexico

There was a new one. Phillipe swam through the azure water twenty metres below the surface. Above him the sun blazed down, its powerful rays lighting up the pure while sand of the seabed below. He powered through the water, his flippers thrusting him towards the resting shapes. Parrot fish, clown fish and red throat emperors darted amongst the many nooks and crannies that provided them with welcome shade and protection from predators.

Phillipe glided towards the most recent arrival. Its lustrous copper sheen would soon become coated with a patina of living organisms, plankton, sea urchins and sausage coral. The world's coral reefs were in serious trouble, with pollution and rising sea temperatures causing massive bleaching. The Cancun project, in the

National Marine Park in Quintana Roo, Mexico, had been launched in 2002 and been expanding ever since. Private donations and

cast-off works of art had allowed the project to blossom, and he estimated that there must have been hundreds of exhibits spread across the ocean floor.

He trod water opposite the new arrivals. There were several themes at work. Women bathing, men fishing and others working in the fields. They were an extraordinary sight, and a welcome addition to the project. He wondered who had donated such a spectacular collection of bronze statues. But at the end of the day he didn't care where the statues came from, he was there to curate the project, not to judge it.

Phillipe looked around at the myriad figures spread across the sea bed. It wouldn't be long before the artificial coral project would begin to bear fruit, and their mission to add another coral reef to the area would achieve its aim. In the soft glow from the overhead sun the many silent statues resembled a kind of underwater Pompeii; as if all of the upturned bronze and stone faces had been frozen in time. He took a couple of pictures for his inventory and headed back up to the diving boat waiting at the surface.

CHAPTER FIFTY-FOUR

The officers stared at the freeze frame that filled the large screen Ward had set up in the catacombs. The frozen screen image of the t'Zand Square statues on the seabed were instantly recognisable to everyone in the room. 'How did you find this?' Nils asked. Ward turned towards his chief. 'I was doing a search on various scrap metal websites to see if I could find pieces of any of the missing statues, to get an idea of how big the operation was. The search engine threw up the Cancun artificial reef project in the National Marine Park in Quintana Roo, Mexico. They populate it with unwanted or donated statues to form an artificial reef. I downloaded a video shot by one of the divers that looks after the installation...that's when I saw this.'

Ward pointed at the t'Zand statue on the screen. 'A

few more months and it would probably have been unrecognisable.' Before Nils could say anything, his phone rang. He picked it up. 'Chief Nils Janssen speaking,' he listened before speaking. 'Okay, thank you.' He put the mobile down. They all looked at him. The expression on his face told them it wasn't good news. 'What is it?' Katja asked.

Nils looked at them. 'Your friends on the case in Venice...'

'What?' Hoog asked.

'They've disappeared. No one has seen them for two days.'

ACKNOWLEDGMENTS

As ever I'd like to thank my ever-faithful Beta readers, Peter Ryan, author of the amazing *Sync City*, available on Amazon.com, producer Venita Ozols-Graham and Rebecca Ortese, audio narrator extraordinaire, and author of multiple titles available on Amazon.com. Also, a huge shout out to the design team at Story Perfect Editing Services. They are responsible for the amazing cover design for Louisiana Blood which won an independent press award, as well as the fabulous Bruges Blood I artwork. Also colossal thanks to Judith Shaw, who edited and corralled my wild grammar horses and helped to make my manuscript fit to be released into the world.

And finally, a massive thanks to my incredibly supportive wife Dorrie, for all of her encouragement during the birth of Louisiana Blood, Bruges Blood I and

Bruges Blood II. I am forever grateful for the time she has granted me to fulfil my ambitions. To all readers everywhere, this is a mercifully Covid 19 free work of fiction, though there is always a historical subtext that foreshadows our imaginary worlds.

ALSO BY MIKE DONALD

If you enjoyed BRUGES BLOOD II, you will love the first in the series LOUISIANA BLOOD and the follow up BRUGES BLOOD I, you may also enjoy my short story anthology, "WHAT HAPPENED NEXT?" All of these are available on Amazon, at Barnes and Noble and in all good bookshops.

Finally, if you loved any of my books and have a moment to spare, I would appreciate a short review on the page where you bought the book. Your help in spreading the word is gratefully appreciated and reviews make a huge difference to helping new readers find the series. Thank you!

If you want to see what I get up to as an author, and news of any up and coming projects, why not head over to my website:

www.bonnymaypublishing.com

You can also drop me an email at:

bonnymaypublishing@gmail.com

Look out for the next thrilling installment with

Duke Lanoix, Chandler Travis, Roxie Rosedale, Jochum Van De Hoog and Katja Blondell. Coming in 2021!

VENICE BLOOD

Beneath the City of water, evil waits

VENICE BLOOD

MIKE DONALD

A Chandler Travis and Duke Lanoix mystery.

Mike Donald worked for the BBC as a sound mixer, wrote for comedy sketch shows, and developed up sitcom ideas. He also worked as a script analyst for a gap finance company and has written many award-winning screenplays. Mike lives in Oxford with his wife, and a power-hungry Terrier named Bonny May Donald.

Bruges Blood is the sequel to Louisiana Blood, the 2019 #1 best seller in mystery, thriller and suspense on Inkshares.com and 1st in the Mill City Press author awards 2018. Louisiana Blood is available on Amazon.com, Amazon.co.uk, and Barnes and Noble online.

Made in the USA
Middletown, DE
27 December 2022

20459810R00184